The DUKE'S DARING DARLING

Victorian Romantic Suspense

by

BAILEY BRISTOL

PRAIRIE MUSE BOOKS INC

2021

THE DUKE'S DARING DARLING
ISBN 978-1-952911-17-0
PRAIRIE MUSE BOOKS INC
Lincoln, Nebraska

DEDICATION
For Laura Landon, who led the way

TRANSLATIONS:

Bozhe moy!	My God!
dragotsennyy	precious
mamochka	mama, mommy
durak	fool
Podozhdite minutku!	Wait a minute!
zaychik	little bunny
nyet	no
da	yes
Pomni svoye obeshchaniye	Remember your promise

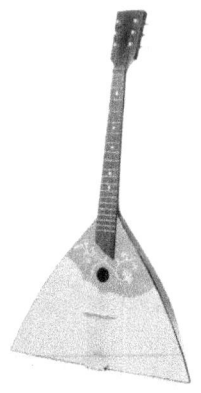

balalaika: Russian guitar

Chapter One

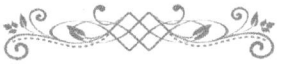

"Whatever you do, stay away from my father."

"You papa? But I not know him."

Rusilla Ivanovna Charkova felt her careful composure slip for a moment. The reality of what they were about to do had just hit her in the noggin. They were slipping into the ball uninvited.

"Oh, you'll know him, alright," Hari scowled. "He's the one who's so skinny he can hardly hold up his chest full of medals."

"He carry it with him?"

Now Rue was truly confused. Her grip on the English language was good, but woefully lacking just when the Russian belle needed it most.

"No, silly. His medals are not *in* a chest, they're *on* his chest. You know. Here."

Hari—or rather Lady Harmony Mountmarten—demurely patted her own budding bosom and Rue realized her mistake. The man would be *wearing* his medals. Just like her own father had. Before he died in that terrible sledding accident outside their dacha two winters past.

A man with a chest full of medals was to be admired. Respected. Not groused over like Hari was doing.

Did she not know how fortunate she was to still have her father in her life?

Rue straightened her shoulders and sighed.

"Yes. I be careful. He never know you come here, sweet Hari. I make promise."

"We're wasting time, girls. Only two more dances before they all leave."

Hari whirled off the bottom step of the servant's back staircase and laid a hand on each girl's shoulder.

"Don't worry! The old men will be in the card room puffing on cigars by now and half of the mothers will be fussing over their darlings in the retiring room. It will just be us, with the few girls who have not yet excused themselves because their chaperones have fallen asleep, of course." Hari whirled back around and pointed to the scattered dancers they could almost see through the butler's pantry door she held slightly ajar. "And them."

With a grand sweep she indicated all the young men gathered here and there.

"So many!" Rue whispered.

"Ready my dears?"

Rue nodded and adjusted the small mask Hari had supplied for each of the three. They were simple, unremarkable masks, chosen specifically to help the girls blend in with those who had actually been invited to the Mountmarten Ball Masque.

Hari looped her arm through Rue's elbow. "Now don't forget, only two dances left in the set. Then we'll meet on the terrace and come back in through the stillroom and up the back stairs.

And voila! Nobody will know we were here!" She dropped her voice to a mischievous whisper. "Except our boys!"

With a joyful nudge, Rue's petite friend moved the threesome forward. There was no other choice but to move with her if Rue was to maintain decorum and not draw undue attention. But halfway into the room she felt Hari draw away with a contented sigh as she took the hand of the fellow who had just swept in to lead her onto the ballroom floor. Judging from Hari's smile, this was the fellow she'd been pining over the whole time they'd been dressing.

Rue's new friend was barely sixteen. Too young for the young earl who had whisked her away. Such a thing would never have been allowed in Odessa. Not at home. Rue reminded herself that of the threesome, she was the only one of a legitimate age to be here. After all, she was eighteen and a half. This would have been her year of coming out, now that her period of mourning had ended. But her mama was still grieving, and when she insisted on the European tour, Rue could hardly refuse.

My sweet flower, please understand me. We must leave these memories that pierce my heart morning to night. Come! We go to Paris. Vienna. London! This you will love.

It had never seemed possible to Rue, loving a place that had no trace of her father in it. She had counted the days until she could return to the Ukraine. But when her mother's lungs succumbed to the strange London air, there was nothing for it but to wait out her recovery. Every day Rue thanked God for the elegant sanatorium Hari's mother had recommended. And for Del's parents who had taken her in. But it was not home, and—

"There you are!"

Rue felt a masculine hand land squarely on her back and

another take hold of her right hand. Without warning she was swept toward the dancing crush.

"You've saved me," a mellow male voice whispered above her ear. "I hope you don't mind terribly."

Rue turned her head as she was being rushed forward and nearly forgot to breathe as her eyes took in the chiseled jaw beneath her captor's mask. But his false smile raised her ire a bit and loosed her tongue a lot.

"*Podozhdite minutku!*"

She stopped in the midst of their flight, causing the fellow to trip rather gracelessly. "Wha—"

"I say stop this minute."

She thrust his hand from her and stepped away from his arm that had lain so very nicely against her back. "I am Rusilla Ivanovna Charkova. And it is you to introduce."

"Roosh—"

"Miss Charkova to you, Englishman. And you are?"

"Ah. Yes. You wish to know with whom you're about to dance."

"It is proper? No?"

"No. I mean, yes. I was most improper. Forgive me, dear lady. Ned Danton, Duke of Wellbury, at your service."

The introduction seemed to help his initial agitation settle, and she watched his broad shoulders expand as he took a calming breath.

"You see, there's someone very special I need to speak with, and with that little twit chasing me all evening I've not had the chance. See there?"

A glance in the direction he pointed explained the situation clearly enough. A gangly, freckled lass paced the fringes of the dance floor like a hen who had misplaced her chick.

The Duke of Wellbury moved closer and spoke in a whisper. "I can't explain, but I really must dance with Lady Georgiana because...well, because."

Rue felt her irritation slide away, banished by the pools of baby blue that stared at her from his masked face with such fervent fever.

"Ah. This iss most important, yes?"

His smile turned sheepish, an expression that would have looked silly on any other male. But on this tall fellow whose chestnut hair swept back from his temples in the most delightful curly waves, it looked positively princely.

"Well, why you not say so in place of first?"

With that, Rue put her hand gracefully into his great palm and stepped into the music. His face flooded with gratitude as she encouraged him to twirl her away.

"Where iss this girl who has chained your heart to hers?"

Now he did actually blush, and Rue felt herself shiver in response to the sweetness of it.

"See?" he whispered. "There, with the white roses in her hair." He paused and growled. "Dancing with that cad Maclyn."

Rue stretched her neck to its fullest swanlike proportion and spied the girl. She was indeed one of the fairest maids in the ballroom. And her partner with the raven hair and fearsome mask was nothing short of heart-stopping.

"I see," Rue sang. "She iss worthy prize."

He beamed.

"Here is vat we do."

Rue lowered her voice and spoke close to the young man's ear. Every few steps he would execute another mad twirl, making her fight hard to keep her train of thought, which wasn't easy with his heavenly strong arms practically lifting her off her feet.

"Really? You think it will work?"

She swatted his shoulder and tilted her head to the side, giving him her most flirtatiously indignant scoff.

"Rusilla say it work, it work! But first we must have, um, how you say, body message. In case your little twit come between again."

"My little twit? I say," her partner laughed. "Is your language always so daring?"

Rue blanched. Twit was another English word she had never heard before. When he had spoken it in the middle of the ballroom she had only assumed it was a proper term meaning a young girl. Perhaps she was mistaken.

"Vat? You say little twit, I say little twit. Vat iss wrong with this?"

He gave her a dubious look, and then a slow smile of pleasure overtook his expression. "What is wrong with this, indeed?"

He swept her into a double turn and it took all her skill to make it look as if she could twirl all night.

"So. Vat iss body message to be? Hm?"

Her partner's mouth twitched in confusion.

"Body message? Oh! You mean, signal?"

"Signal! Yes, signal is vat I mean to say."

"Ah! A signal. For..."

"Well, vat if you talk to this Georgi but bad boy come back to bother? You need my help you signal me. See? Like, um, signal that mean *come now to help me*. Yes? Like dis, maybe, da?" She let go of her partner's right hand and tugged at her ear. "Ven I see you fingers pull on you ear, I come. With haste. I fly to your rescue from unwanted intrude. Yes?"

"Ah. Yes. That could come in handy."

"Yes! Use you handy to pull you ear."

She wasn't certain why the young man laughed so heartily at her comment, but at least he seemed to understand the need for signals.

"Now," she continued, "waltz almost at end. Quick-quick, move close to your lady. See?" She leaned her body weight in the direction of the fellow's sweetheart.

Without hesitation, the young Duke of Wellbury executed a breathtaking triple turn. Rusilla felt the scintillating pull of the turn and the answering pressure from his broad hand on her back. He was so strong, yet so very graceful.

It would be a pity to let him go.

But if the plan was to work, she had to, although for a moment she contemplated what might happen if she pretended to miss the musical timing and stayed locked in his arms.

Of course, that would be unkind. She'd seen the hopeful look in his eyes when he'd understood that her plan just might work. She couldn't disappoint the fellow now that he was so close to winning his lady. That would be more than selfish. It would be downright mean-spirited.

Swallowing her own desire and preparing herself for the next moment, Rusilla drew a deep breath, lit her face with her broadest smile, and sang her command.

"Now!"

~~~

Ned Danton, Duke of Wellbury, watched Rusilla Charkova execute a perfect pirouette as she skated right into the arms of the fellow who had claimed the current waltz with Lady Georgiana Rathmore. The delectable Georgiana covered the intrusion prettily, as he knew she would, but he swept in to catch her up as if rescuing her from some dire fate.

Surprisingly, the brazen exchange had not caused a stir. And if it had, the girl who called herself Rusilla had assured him it would be she who was found at fault and he who would come out the hero.

"Ned! Whatever are you doing?"

Georgiana was annoyed, which momentarily threatened to unnerve him. The sharp edge to her tone was a startling contrast to the Russian girl's *shooshing*, lyrical voice. Ned had been mesmerized by the exotic girl's full lips that seemed to lay each word on its own bed of silk. His paramour's lips, on the other hand, were pursed in displeasure.

But this was Georgi. *His* Georgi. Smart, sassy, independent Georgi. What did it matter that her voice wasn't as lilting as the Russian girl's? He'd always planned to propose marriage to his childhood friend. Some day. But Maclyn's attentions tonight had somehow thrown him off the ledge of procrastination. If it would keep her out of Devan Maclyn's way, he would ask her tonight.

"I couldn't go another minute watching you twirl away with that fellow," Ned groused.

Her answering swat landed on his shoulder in perfect time with the final note of the waltz.

"*Balderdash.* You can't possibly be jealous of the Earl of Charleton, Neddie. He's a complete rake!"

Ned watched the flush begin to fade from her cheeks as Lady Georgiana gathered her composure. It took a moment for her words to sink in, but when they did, his heart made a bit of a leap in his chest. She didn't care for the cad!

Yet.

But what might happen if the blackguard continued to woo her as he had tonight?

Now was the time to act. He cast his eyes about the room in search of the nearest exit.

"Let's take the air, shall we?" he asked, already guiding her toward the terrace.

"Ned, really, I do need a glass—"

Momentarily flustered, Ned considered refreshment. But if no footman magically appeared with a tray of champagne flutes he might have to leave her side, which he most assuredly was not willing to do.

Even as the thought arose, he was spared the dilemma. At that very moment, a footman passed just beyond Ned's elbow, enabling him to pluck up a flute without missing a step as he steered Georgiana toward the open terrace door.

Within seconds they had crossed to the steps and found their way down to a muted pool of light. Georgiana allowed him to turn her toward him, but her pretty pout still concerned him.

"Don't be angry with me, Georgi."

He held out the champagne like a peace offering and she accepted it almost greedily. He placed his hands on her soft upper arms, letting his thumbs glide slowly back and forth. "Do say you'll forgive me," he begged, and instantly regretted the pleading he heard in his voice.

Georgiana turned her head to the side, sending the tantalizing scent of white roses across his nose. She tilted her chin to take a sip of champagne, letting the soft tendrils of her blonde curls drift maddeningly across the back of his hand that still had not released her.

Now she looked at him from the corner of her eye. "We have plenty of time to dance, Neddie. What's the rush all of the sudden?"

"Rush? What rush? I've waited the whole evening."

"Well, then, let's go dance."

He'd just managed to get her away from the crowd and she wanted to scoot right back to it.

"Neddie?"

He heard the quiet stamp of her small slipper that underscored her impatience.

"Not yet," he breathed. Ned reached a hand to turn her chin toward him. As she pivoted, Ned dropped both hands to take her free hand in his. As she drew her next breath, he lowered himself to one knee.

"Dearest Georgi, we've been perfectly matched friends since our days in the nursery garden. There's no one in the world I know better than I know you. No one with whom I am more completely at home."

He took a fortifying breath.

"Lady Georgiana Rathmore, will you do me the immense honor of becoming my wife?"

In his daydreams he'd envisioned this moment repeatedly since early youth. Georgiana's lush lips would spread in surprise, then stretch into the glorious smile that never failed to give his heart a hitch. She would emit a small squeal of surprise, draw him up from his knees, and cry, "Yes, yes, yes!"

And then she would let him kiss her.

But as it all played out mentally for him, Ned suddenly realized she hadn't said a word.

"Georgi?"

He rose to face her, relieved that at least she'd not pulled her hand away from his.

"Georgi?"

She dropped her gaze. Then, without looking back up at him, she swung her head toward the upper terrace, toward the door through which they'd just exited. Before she turned back, he saw what it was that filled her eyes.

Longing.

It was longing.

Not for him, not for marriage, but longing. Longing for what? The dancing crush? Or mere escape?

Even as he wrestled with that question, Georgiana turned back to him.

"You've spoken to my father?"

Ned felt unsettled by her cool statement. "Of course, darling! That is, not directly, but when I wrote and asked if I might see him immediately upon his return, he suggested my uncle and I meet with him tomorrow morning early. He seemed very pleased, Georgi. He said he'd been hoping to speak with me, as well. I'm certain he knows my intention."

She ventured a polite smile.

"It's true. He does think very highly of you. So perhaps I shall marry you, Your Grace. But..."

Her final word hung in the air, brutally twisting Ned's stomach into a slow knot. Before it could rise into his throat and turn him into a stuttering schoolboy, he pressed.

"But what, Georgi. But what?"

She sighed. "But only if we wait until after."

What was she saying? "After what—?"

"Don't press me, Neddie. You'll know tomorrow morning." Now she gave him her look that said she knew better than he. "Just promise me you're willing to wait." She gave him a look that never failed to set his limbs to tingling. "You always give me what I want."

Of all the emotions he'd expected to feel tonight, crestfallen was not one of them. But that's what he truly felt. Crestfallen. He'd made his bold move and thrown himself at his sweetheart's feet only to find that she was less than enthusiastic. But *perhaps* was better than *no*, and that thought did make his heart dance the tiniest bit.

"Of course." Ned swallowed hard. "Not until after."

His hand came to her cheek. This was what he had wanted, wasn't it? His tidy future was all planned out, and Georgi lay at the center of it. She was for the most part sensible, highly respected, calm in a crisis, frugal, a perfect hostess. A perfect duchess. And her foresight was uncanny. What a pair they would make! Ned let his eyes slip away from hers and settle on her rosy lips. When they twitched slightly, Georgiana caught her bottom lip between her teeth. She could have done nothing more alluring.

"Georgi," he whispered, and lowered his head to taste this night's treasure.

But just as he came close enough to detect the subtle hint of champagne on her sweet breath, a musical laugh cut the air. It came from just beyond the foliage that sheltered them, distracting Ned and spoiling the moment.

Their privacy had not been invaded, but the moment had been broken, nevertheless. Ned listened for the couple to move slightly away before glancing in their direction without claiming his kiss. He recognized the lavishly ornamented hair of the Russian girl disappearing into the garden. She kept turning her head to look adoringly into the eyes of her escort.

Ned froze. Those adoring looks were being showered upon the same black-haired mongrel who had been monopolizing Georgi all evening. He was the most notorious rakehell in the district. Had ruined more maids than half the army of France. And his head was now bent close—too close—to Miss Charkova's.

He happened to know the girl had only been in London six weeks, not nearly long enough for a newcomer to know the man's reputation. Not long enough to know that just being seen leaving the ballroom on Devan Maclyn's arm could be enough to destroy her. And it would be his fault!

Why hadn't he warned her to elude the Earl of Charleton as soon as Ned and his sweetheart were safely away? But he'd said nothing. Instead, Ned had let her play right into the man's clutches just so he could capture Georgiana.

If he had any honor at all, he had to do something for the girl. And quickly.

Ned turned his face toward Georgi and was stricken dumb by her upturned face and closed eyes. She still waited for her kiss. It should be a slow kiss, tender, plied with just the right amount of want.

But Rusilla was disappearing into the dark.

"Georgi, I...that is...forgive me, but...I'm sorry."

Her eyes flew open, but Ned didn't see that. He was already running.

Chapter Two

"He iss oaf like bear!"

The three girls had collapsed on Rue's bed and were recounting their precious twenty minutes at the Mountmarten Ball Masque. Last night had been completely enchanting. Until the last two minutes, that is.

"Whatever do you mean?" Hari sounded surprised at Rue's pronouncement. "The Duke of Wellbury is ever so popular with the ladies. And he's so gallant! Or so I've heard."

"I not know this word *gallant*, but if it mean rude like bully, then yes. Ned Danton iss *gallant*." She sat up and carefully removed the silver ribbon that had stayed entwined in her hair through the night. "He dare to pull me from garden! Just when my beautiful Devan iss to kiss!"

Now Del sat up. "Wait. You were dancing with the duke but you went into the garden with Devan Maclyn? The Earl of Charleton? Rue, you must never do such a thing!"

"But why? His dark green eyes, mmm, they make this heart tickety-tickety." She touched her bosom and sighed.

In a graceful move she slid from the bed and twirled to the

window. "You young. You not understand how heart can know this."

"Well, I think it's terribly romantic," Hari trilled as she rose from the foot of the bed. "And I happen to know exactly where Devan Maclyn, Earl of Charleton, will be this very afternoon."

Rue whirled back around. "Today? Iss true? How you know this?"

Hari plopped down on a pink tufted chaise. "My Jeremy will be there, too."

Rue dropped to her knees on the floor beside Hari. "But where? Tell Rue!"

"Parliament Square," Hari said, smug with satisfaction. "At the unveiling of the new statue. Edward Smith-Stanley, fourteenth Earl of Derby or some such thing. Ancestor of Jeremy and Maclyn. Who knew they were cousins?"

The revelation sent a flutter rampaging down Rue's spine. Tomorrow. She could see Devan Maclyn again tomorrow. "What time?" she whispered.

"What?"

"What time iss statue?"

"Oh! Precisely at two o'clock. Which means we can be there for an hour and get back in time for tea."

Rue's mind flitted elsewhere while the two younger girls nattered on about how they would get to Parliament Square and how they might elude Del's governess. Rue, on the other hand, was more interested in figuring out how she might find another chance to be alone with the very dashing Earl of Charleton. Whether the nosy old duke liked it or not!

~~~

"Step lively, boy."

After a restless night, Ned and his churning thoughts were on their way to meet with Georgiana's father. On any other day, keeping up with his uncle would not have been a problem. It was most often Ned who found himself waiting for his uncle to catch up. But today he found his own footsteps lagging. What would Georgi's father expect him to say? How could he best relay his intention to make Georgi happy for the rest of her life? And why the bloody hell was it so hard to come up with convincing reasons?

"Keep up, son. Rathmore is waiting. And remember, you're the Duke of Wellbury. You hold all the cards. Don't forget that."

Ah. Yes. Duke of Wellbury.

He'd carried the title for less than a year, inheriting it just after his twenty-second birthday. It hadn't taken hold in his conscious mind yet. It seemed to him the Duke of Wellbury would always be his father. But illness had changed that ten months ago in a cruelly harsh manner, and the title now had a new home in Ned Danton.

In truth, his father had seemed to carry the title in his heart, but for Ned it was still too new. Too big. Too daunting to do anything but weigh heavily on his shoulders.

His Uncle Trenton, the Earl of Malmsey, wasn't really his uncle. He was the late Duke's best friend and fellow survivor of the Napoleonic wars. He was now Ned's mentor, and Ned could not have been more grateful for the kindness his father's friend had shown him.

You hold all the cards.

Today the good fellow meant to bolster Ned's courage, but Ned would be damned if he knew what cards he held. Aside from inheriting a respected title he had little else to say for himself. Except that he was a bungling fool. He'd certainly bungled things royally with Georgi the night before.

"Lady Georgiana!"

Uncle Trenton's booming voice jolted Ned from his ruminations. Georgi was descending the stairs, radiant in a peach morning gown. Ned's slow grin began to dispel his gloom. Perhaps he hadn't bollixed things up so badly after all. Her smile could only be described as adoring.

Slivers of what he decided to think of as excitement skittered across his heart as he watched her float like a goddess down the grand staircase. But a moment later they were dashed away.

Her smile wasn't directed toward him. Georgi's head was turned slightly, casting her glorious welcome on a rumpled fellow who had just stepped from her father's study. As he moved into the entry hall, Georgi quickened her step. But like the proper young lady she was, she stopped at the bottom of the stairs to greet her father's guests.

"Lord Malmsey. Your Grace." She dipped prettily in turn to Uncle Trenton and to Ned as she greeted them. "Good morning to you both. Father is waiting in his study."

Ned wished she had called him by name. The way it slipped from her pert lips never failed to spread heat across his chest. But if Georgi was anything, she was a proper miss, and if any day was a time for propriety, it was today.

Ned managed a smile. "Good morning to you, my lady."

The odd-looking fellow came even with them and reached out a hand toward Georgi. Now Ned could see his chiseled features and bronzed skin, a man of the outdoors—rugged, muscled, charming in an offhand, natural way.

Georgiana made a somewhat enraptured response, and Ned could only watch as the man winked at her then gallantly bent to kiss the back of her graceful hand.

Why the hell hadn't *he* done that, Ned wondered?

Ned could almost feel the brutal kick he mentally directed toward his own backside. He'd grown up with Georgiana. She'd been Georgi since as early as he could speak. He'd played in her nursery and she in his. It had never in his wildest imagining occurred to him to kiss her hand as he would any other young lady of similar station. Or for that matter, wink at her during a formal introduction.

"Your Grace? Lord Malmsey? May I present Solomon Rockefeller."

Abandoning propriety, Georgi slipped her arm through Rockefeller's elbow and drew him toward Ned. "Solomon, I'm pleased for you to meet William Trenton, Earl of Malmsey, and His Grace Ned Danton, Duke of Wellbury."

"Good day, gentlemen," the fellow barked in an accent that could only be described as colonial. "Shall we?"

He swept an arm toward Lord Rathmore's study, but Ned was simply rooted to the floor.

An American? Georgiana was casting all her sweet attention on this American?

~~~

Once they entered Rathmore's study and had shared the obligatory cigar, Rathmore explained the reason for his invitation. It did involve Georgi, but in a way that set Ned reeling.

"Let me see if I understand you correctly, sir." Ned cleared his throat, marveling at the fact that he could even speak after what he'd just heard. "Georgiana will accompany you to Egypt."

"Yes, by jingo, the girl has recently taken a fascination with archeology. Should be a tremendous experience for her." He cast Georgi a fond look that was clearly laced with pride.

Ned swallowed hard. He somehow doubted the fascination was as much with archeology as it was with Rockefeller.

"Yes, of course. And you're asking that, in your absence, I should provide escort for your younger daughter, Lady Gilda, upon occasion when she has need of it."

"Indeed I am. I can think of no one I'd trust with greater confidence, Your Grace." The Earl of Rathmore rubbed his chin thoughtfully. "I doubt it will be on occasion, though. More like once or twice a week."

Ned blanched. He'd just been shackled to a fourteen-year-old for who knew how long, while her father and sister traipsed around Egypt. It certainly wasn't how he'd foreseen his immediate future.

"It will be my honor, sir," Ned said as he straightened to assume a pose he'd often seen his father strike when forced to agree to some distasteful thing. "But I wish to speak to you on a private matter." He swallowed hard. "I wish to declare my intentions—"

"Good show!" Rathmore clapped him on the shoulder. "Plenty of time for that, son."

Ned fought for the right words to make his case, but Georgiana's father was already leading him toward the door.

Georgi had not even followed them into the entry hall to bid him farewell.

Neither had Rockefeller.

The writing was clearly on the wall. Georgi had eyes for one man and one man alone. And it wasn't Ned.

The carriage ride home became excruciating as he struggled to force his dashed hopes to the back of his mind. It didn't help that his uncle prattled on endlessly about nothing. It was all well and good for him. He was a widower, with no lack of adoring spinsters competing for his arm. But for Ned the sudden turn of events meant his future was nowhere near as settled as he'd thought. *Bloody hell.* He'd been reduced to a mere escort. For a mere child. How humiliating.

Ned thought he'd been invited to Lord Rathmore's home to discuss his intention to marry the earl's daughter.

But no.

Oh, no.

Lord Rathmore was merely looking for an escort for his younger daughter while he whisked the love of Ned's life off to Egypt and threw Georgi into the arms of some American cowboy archeologist so they could fall in love in the bowels of some godforsaken pyramid.

But enough! Ned aborted his mental rant. It was only making him sick at heart, and he refused to succumb to it. He'd promised Georgi he'd wait, and he would. End of story.

Or perhaps not. Ned's heart caved a bit. Georgi hadn't actually asked him to delay marriage until she returned. She'd merely asked him to wait until she returned to discuss the *possibility* of it.

Meanwhile, he'd be at Georgi's sister Gilda's beck and call. Ned sighed. At the very least he should be able to get weekly updates on Georgi's wellbeing.

After a miserable afternoon of assessing his dilemma, Ned

came to the conclusion that there was no antidote for having his heart brutalized. He would simply have to buck up and get through the next few weeks.

But first he had to get himself to Parliament Square for the dedication of the statue. It wouldn't do to appear he'd simply slunk away.

CHAPTER THREE

THE CROWD WAS GROWING QUICKLY in Parliament Square when the girls arrived.

"There it is!" Hari pointed happily to the two dignitaries' stands set up on either side of the draped statue about to be unveiled.

Del's governess had been such a Nervous Nelly as they approached the square that all three girls were prompted to utter all sorts of promises to stay right by her side.

"Draw the carriage over there, Samuel. We should like to enjoy the sunshine while we watch the festivities." Del winked at the girls and popped open her parasol to offer shade for the ageing spinster.

Once the carriage was situated in a pleasant spot, the girls focused on the governess.

"This is wonderful, Miss Thorndike! No need to even leave the carriage. See? We can view everything from here." Del's reassuring voice seemed to placate the woman. "Why, I will wager we might even hear some of the speeches."

"Don't even think of leaving the carriage, ladies," Miss

Thorndike admonished.

"We wouldn't think of it!" the girls chorused.

"This is a moment in history, young ladies. You'll never forget that you were here when this statue was unveiled. Why, it will adorn Parliament Square for centuries to come."

With that, the governess began extolling the virtues of Edward Smith-Stanley, fourteenth Earl of Derby. But as the sun's pleasant rays began to warm the woman's shoulders, her voice became slower and slower. The girls remained quiet as little mice as they watched her pause for a moment, mumble a bit, then slowly drift off to sleep.

"Give me your parasol," Hari whispered.

When Rue handed it over, Hari carefully wedged the stem of the parasol into the carriage door handle, so Miss Thorndike wouldn't be awakened by the sun's glare.

"She sleeps!" Rue whispered.

"Didn't I tell you?" Del giggled.

"Shhhh!" Hari admonished. "Be quiet now. And for heaven's sake, don't rock the carriage!"

That, of course, was easier said than done. But the three determined girls managed it, and within minutes they were on the ground holding hands and darting through the crowd.

Already Rue could see the special guests ascending the dais. As she hurried along following Hari's lead, two young fellows standing near the podium captured her attention. When the crowd parted a bit and she managed a second look, Rue recognized the taller of the two.

Devan Maclyn.

She'd know that beautiful raven hair anywhere.

Recognition threw her heartbeat into a most unruly clatter.

Maclyn wore his top hat exceedingly well, though at a rather rakish, jaunty angle. And the cut of his cutaway was impeccable. But that was no more than she would have expected.

Eager to be closer, she pushed the girls forward, and at last they broke through the gathered throng to take places in the front, halfway between the dais and the statue.

"My hat was knocked askew!" Hari turned frantically toward Rue as she tugged at her beautiful new birds-egg blue bonnet.

"Let me to fix," Rue said as she plucked up the blue satin ribbons. In a moment she had deftly reseated the hat, tucked a loose curl back in place, and tied a perfect bow beneath Hari's chin.

"Now you perfect," she pronounced.

"Nearly as perfect as you, my lovely," a deep voice crooned.

Rue turned and fought the fainting sensation that threatened to send her into a swoon right there on the street. Devan Maclyn stood a mere two feet away, devouring her with his eyes.

In an instant her hands seemed to lose all sense. They wanted to tug at her skirts, check her hat, wander across her curls looking for errant wisps, plump her bosom, scratch her nose. It took every bit of restraint not to allow it. Instead she kept her hands demurely buried in the folds of her apple green skirt as she gave a small curtsy.

"My lord! You are nice to see!"

Drat!

Rue heard her own misplaced words and shuddered. What was it about this fellow that sent all her good senses winging away with her scant English in tow?

"You're just what we need, Miss Charkova."

"Vat?"

"On the dais. Take a look up there." He swung his hand toward the small grandstand where dignitaries were beginning to take their seats. "Look at all that black!"

Rue giggled. "It look like too many blackbird fight over same tree."

"Exactly! Which is why you are desperately needed." He turned to Hari and Del who were gaping at him. "I must borrow the beautiful Miss Charkova just until the ceremony is over." He doffed his hat, swept it in a gallant bow, and pulled Rue's arm through the crook of his elbow. "I shall return her to you unscathed!"

The wide-eyed girls could only nod.

An instant later, Maclyn moved Rue to the dais, helped her up the wobbly platform steps, chased one of the gentlemen from his chair, and seated Rue upon it. She was now one of only three ladies in the midst of this bevvy of black, and the other two women wore widow's weeds. With a bow, Maclyn turned and moved behind her chair.

Rue grinned. She could see everything from here. How lucky she was that Devan Maclyn had found her in the crowd. Her heart was aflutter with the excitement, her smile unstoppable.

"Thank you, my lord! We see all things now!"

Rue felt a friendly pat and heard the Earl of Charleton's amused chuckle. But a moment later his hand slid beneath the flounces at her shoulder and his fingers gave a squeeze that she could only describe as provocative. Without thinking, she shrank from it. But that only served to strengthen the earl's grip.

Her earlier thrill was suddenly dampened by the unseemly behavior.

"Just smile, Rusilla. Act like you belong here."

His mouth was just centimeters from the curls at her ears, his breath evoking unspeakable sensations as he whispered. Whether she wanted to bat him away or beg him to speak again she could not tell.

Recognizing that thought suddenly made her feel incredibly wicked and she knew that it was wrong for her to stay where he'd planted her. She really ought to get away before the ceremony began.

But as she shifted to rise from her chair, his hands exerted a gentle pressure and his thumbs began circling near the base of her neck. While the high ruffled neckline of her summery gown surely hid his scandalous attentions, it did nothing to dampen the scintillating feeling that his gifted hands created.

It was so relaxing, so satisfying, so—

Rue was mortified at her own reaction.

What if someone saw?

Embarrassment set her fumbling for her parasol. She'd open it in his face. That would teach him a lesson. But in a flash she had to discard the idea. She'd left her parasol in the carriage with the slumbering governess.

"You're not smiling, my pretty," Maclyn crooned again, sending even more waves of devilish air tumbling into her ear.

"Rue must go now. Iss not right to be here. Please—" She turned her head to the side and collided with his finger that pressed against her lips, shushing her.

"The ceremony is starting."

Rue swallowed her objection and turned a politely composed face toward the crowd. As the first speaker droned on, Maclyn continued his scandalous attentions.

Bozhe moy! How she hated his magical hands! And the sun...

oh, the sun.

Rue stiffened her spine, determined not to sway with the rhythm of his expert kneading, but her lazy eyes blinked heavily as the world about her began to recede. In that same instant she suddenly realized she was being watched. Among the lords on the opposite dais was the fellow she'd rescued the other night. The fellow who had twirled her about the ballroom so magnificently. The fellow who had dragged her away from the Earl of Charleton at the Mountmarten's garden gate just as she was about to be kissed.

And he was staring at her. Quite rudely, she thought. Or was that just her embarrassment at being caught in this rather indelicate situation that had her conscience squirming?

She risked another look, hoping she had mistaken the identity of her watcher.

But there was no mistake. It was definitely Ned Danton. His Grace the Duke of Wellbury. And he appeared to be shaking his head. In an instant the scowl on his face woke every sleepy sense and Rue suddenly realized the picture she must be presenting.

Sudden awareness jolted her fully to her senses, even as her chin lifted with indignant affront. Rue turned her head away and fought her quivering chin. Was he truly expressing his disapproval of her behavior?

With great stealth she turned just enough to see him from the corner of her eye.

He was still staring her down, as if he could send a message across time and space, which of course he could not.

"Be still, my pet." Maclyn pinched her shoulder harder. "Be patient," he whispered. "I have something for you in my carriage as soon as this idiot ceases his drivel."

Rue swallowed. The earl's seedy actions had revealed his true nature. Now his words validated it. If he thought she would accompany him to his carriage, he had seriously misjudged Rusilla Ivanovna Charkova.

Once she brutally assessed what was going on, she knew she really must put a stop to it. But how? Everyone was looking in her general direction. Any untoward move would draw their focus off the speaker and onto her. That would be decidedly uncomfortable. How would she explain to her mother that she'd let a fellow touch her in unseemly ways? And not just in public, but before half the scions of London Society!

During the applause after the first speech, Rue knew she had to try something to shake his unwelcome attentions. Anything. If she did nothing now, things might only get worse. Maclyn might even think she was consenting to his naughtiness. That would never do.

She leaned back and waggled a crook'd finger toward the young earl, beckoning him to lean down to hear what she had to say while the crowd roared their approval of the speaker. When he was close enough that she could speak without danger of the men around her hearing her words, she issued her instruction with the sweetest of smiles.

"I smile for you, Devan Maclyn. I be pretty thing for you. But touch me more times, I scream." She cocked her head slightly so she could see his reaction and he couldn't miss her sarcastic smile. "Rue iss good screamer, make you look very, very bad, eh?" She raised both eyebrows. "Hm?"

Maclyn looked surprised, and then a rakish grin spread across his face. "Bad, eh? I do believe I like the sound of that, Miss Charkova."

He slid one hand across her upper arm and then squeezed, but for the remainder of the event he did not so much as touch her.

She hazarded a look across the gallery. The Duke of Wellbury was no longer scowling quite so fiercely.

Rue smiled to herself. For a while she had been worried that this man who had so captivated her was going to be trouble. But now she knew Devan Maclyn was nothing more than a big old flirt.

~~~

Ned made an effort to unclench his fists.

He was trapped here in front of half the world, seated with the other designated attendees from the House of Lords. It seemed he'd been sitting for hours listening to droning speeches, while Miss Rusilla Charkova made a spectacle of herself.

How could she let Maclyn do that in public?

Devan Maclyn was the bastard son of the old earl—the late Earl of Charleton—who never knew his wife had cuckolded him. But Maclyn had been taunted about it since his days in boarding school and it had turned him into a bully and a reprobate. Nobody in Society would engage in business with the man, which forced him into other, more shady ventures.

But Miss Charkova couldn't know that.

Minutes ticked by in agonizing slowness, taunting him with the vision from which he could not drag his eyes. There on the rostrum sat Miss Charkova like a radiant flower in the middle of a dark forest, surrounded by men easily twice her age. Except for the cad, of course. Her glorious auburn hair glinted with gold highlights in the midday sun. Her demure posture presented a most fetching picture, with her gloved hands clasped prettily in her lap.

That was certainly no surprise. He'd seen nothing but grace and ebullient poise from her the evening before.

But the longer he watched, the more Ned came to believe that the smile she'd adopted when he first saw her speak to Maclyn now seemed to be frozen on her lips. And if he was not mistaken, the earl's hands had never left her shoulders. As if he held her captive.

It was a dastardly thing to do.

Ned looked about and was somewhat mollified to see that the crowd's attention did not seem to be on Miss Charkova.

As the crowd broke into cheering applause following the conclusion of the first speech, Ned noticed a subtle change. It was as if an invisible wand of control had passed from the earl to the young lady, and Ned felt himself relax the smallest bit. If he wasn't mistaken, Maclyn had been given his comeuppance by the young miss. The earl stood at attention now, his hands clasped behind his back. Very much like a reprimanded schoolboy.

Ned stifled a laugh. Had she warned him off? It was an agreeable thought, and begrudgingly, he felt his respect for the pretty Russian girl escalate a notch. She was nobody's toy, it seemed, and he rather liked that. But she'd taken far too long setting Maclyn straight, if indeed that is what she had done.

By the time the drape over the statue was finally withdrawn and the crowd roared, Ned had decided the girl had her situation well in hand.

If he read her expression correctly, she disapproved of Maclyn's attentions as much as Ned did. But as the applause died away, she rose, laughing merrily at something Maclyn had said.

Had he been wrong? Did she favor the lecher's attentions? Or did she perhaps not recognize them for what they were?

And why the hell did he even care? Her behavior was none of his business.

The scene at the garden gate when he'd rescued her at the Mountmarten ball masque played through his mind. He was certain he'd been clear as he explained why she must be wary of the fellow. Had she ignored him? Or perhaps her command of the King's English was just sketchy enough that he had not made himself understood to her.

If that was the case, then he certainly *did* care.

Ned took another step forward, just as Miss Charkova stepped away from Maclyn's offered arm and began to descend from the dais without assistance.

Brava, there's a good girl.

His admiration heightened as he began to hear her chiming laughter and the *shooshing* of her lyrical Russian dialect. *Bloody hell*, she was play-acting. He was sure of it. What a saucy little minx! She was playing the part of an amiable companion. But each time Maclyn closed on her, she managed to mince away.

As Ned drew nearer, the same thing happened again. Miss Charkova angled herself out of reach of Maclyn's searching hand. But as she tried her clever maneuver a third time, the crowd jostled her right into Maclyn's grasp.

That action stopped Ned cold. Maclyn had gripped her hard enough to whip her around. So hard, in fact that shock spread across her face. Shock that an instant later turned to alarm.

And then they were swallowed by the crowd.

With little concern for those around him, Ned surged forward. Each time he thought he spied Maclyn's top hat, it turned out to be someone else. He'd embarrassed himself three times before he heard her small shriek from behind the nearest carriage.

A half dozen sprinting steps brought him around it.

"Miss Charkova!"

Ned muscled his way beyond a knot of spectators and broke through the other side just in time to see Maclyn pull open the door of his carriage. With his view blocked, Ned couldn't be sure whether or not the girl was resisting. He made a determined surge and burst into the open, just in time to see Maclyn take Miss Charkova rather roughly by the arm.

"Miss Charkova?"

She turned toward him and gasped. And as he stood debating his next move, she raised her free hand and tugged at her ear.

That was all he needed. Ned strode forward.

"Good day, Maclyn. Nice ceremony. I see you've been looking after Miss Charkova." His words came in a rush meant to distract. As he spoke, he extended his hand, as if expecting Maclyn to shake it. But the moment Maclyn let go of the girl, Ned stepped between them. "No need to see the lady home."

He tipped his hat without waiting for acknowledgment from Maclyn and offered his arm to Miss Charkova. "Shall we?"

The girl turned, launching an angelic expression in his direction. Still play-acting. But he noted that her smile had slipped a bit.

Casting good manners aside, Ned took Rusilla Charkova by the arm and drew her into the crowd. He didn't risk looking back to see what it was the cretin struck with his walking stick, but the impact was loud enough that Ned prayed no one had been on the receiving end.

"Miss Charkova, I thought I made it quite clear last evening that the Earl of Charleton is one with whom you must never, I repeat *never*, associate."

"Ha!" She scoffed, then pitched forward as he dragged her around a lamppost. "Ack!"

She failed to regain her footing and would have landed face first on the cobbles had he not caught her up. They both huffed as they regained their balance. Once steady, she tried to step away, but he held her fast. Her gaze pierced his own as her wide eyes assessed his commitment to detaining her.

"He iss Earl of Charleton is he not?" Her expression seemed less certain than her words. "Earl is gentleman, yes? Gentleman iss not bad man."

Ned gritted his teeth. "You don't know him."

"Ha! You are Duke. Duke iss gentleman. You bad man, too? Hm? How I know?"

She turned, expecting him to let her go.

And he should.

But he couldn't.

"I'll let you go, but not until you promise not to be seen with that unscrupulous rake again."

She opened her mouth, ready to spit her retort in his face, then stopped.

"Vat iss this word, un-soup...un-screw..."

Ned watched her struggle with the word and the humor of it had anger sliding away like water over the mill pond sluice.

"Unscrupulous."

He pronounced it carefully, syllable by syllable.

She tried once again and mastered the word. "Unscrupulous. Ha! There! New word, yes? Vat does this unscrupulous mean?"

Enthralled with learning a new word, Rusilla Charkova seemed to forget her own anger and tucked her hand into the crook of his elbow. As she did so, the neckline of her pretty gown fell away, nearly baring her bosom. The beast had torn her frock.

"Miss Charkova, you—"

He let his eyes communicate what he was too embarrassed to say, and as she yanked the torn fabric into place with both hands she cried out softly.

"Oh! Oh no! *Bozhe moy!*"

Ned looked around hastily, then gently led her beyond the corner into the ally where shopkeepers and hawkers had set up their stalls. Among the heaps of clothing on display in a rag-man's stall was a bright red shawl covered with colorful embroidery. It would appeal to any gypsy girl, but was hardly suitable. Still, there were no other options, so he grabbed it up, tossed a coin at the shopkeeper, and threw it around her shoulders. She hugged it, drawing it tightly around her.

"Gently. Let it fall naturally," he coaxed.

After a bit more prodding, she began to relax, letting the garish thing fall about her as it was meant to while still satisfying her modesty. The shawl was long, with lavish dark fringe extending nearly to her toes. As she moved, it practically danced with her, conforming to her petite figure in a most tantalizing way.

His hands reached for her of their own accord, gathering up the long tails and drawing them into a loose knot across her chest. She shivered as she lifted a pretty hand to touch the knot, then lifted her eyes to his. Gratitude spilled from them, and he had all the thanks he needed.

But in a flash her expression turned to embarrassment as her cheeks flamed red as the shawl.

"Everyone know this shame!" She choked as if she were about to spill a river of tears.

"I doubt anyone noticed, Miss Charkova."

"But they will talk! They—"

He moved his head closer to hers. "Look." He pointed to the crowd gathered around an old fellow who was strutting around bellowing a drunken song. "They'll all be talking about old Lord Penhurst tonight. They'll have forgotten all about you," he lied.

As he spoke Ned used an index finger to draw an 'X' across his left lapel.

"Cross my heart."

He chuckled at the look of consternation she gave him.

"What means 'cross my heart'?" she asked.

"Well, it simply means 'I promise'. Now, are we ready?"

Without another word, he guided her back to the street where she fell easily into their former conversation.

"You not tell me this word. This unscrupulous." She pronounced it perfectly. "Vat it mean?"

Ned laughed to himself. Her mood could change faster than the weather in Wales. He moved them forward as he contemplated a story that might explain the word to this inquisitive Russian beauty.

"Well. It's like this. Let's say that a man needs money."

She was hanging on his words now.

"And let's say he knows a woman whose husband is very, very rich."

"Yes?"

"So he tricks the woman into meeting him in an unsavory part of town."

"Wait minute of one. What iss unsavory?"

"Bad. Dangerous."

"Oh."

"And he keeps her there late into the night."

"No." Her intake of breath told him she understood very clearly the implications of that.

"Yes. Then he sends a note to her husband that he finds the man's wife delightful, that he wishes to spend a few more days with her."

"This iss terrible."

"Yes, it is. But the note also says if the husband sends a hundred pounds back with the courier, he will bring the man's wife home before anyone discovers she is missing."

"But if husband not send monies?"

"The unscrupulous man will make a show of delivering her to her front step in a disheveled state at midday. And kiss her. On the lips." He had no idea why he had to add that last part, but she seemed preoccupied by his earlier words.

"Shoveled?"

"Disheveled. With, um, with her clothing wrinkled and her, um, hair all mussed."

"This bad man should not do this!"

"I should say not. It would be an unscrupulous deed."

"This means unscrupulous? The beast!"

"Indeed. The beast. And that is exactly what Devan Maclyn

is. An unscrupulous beast. He preys on women whose reputations are pristine and he threatens to ruin them."

That stopped the beautiful girl mid-step. Her hand came slowly to her mouth and she looked up at him, wide-eyed.

"But he iss so pretty. How could I know this?" She whirled on him in panic. "*Bozhe moy!* I sit with this man, this unscrupulous man, in front of everyone today! Oh *Bozhe moy! Bozhe moy! Bozhe moy!*"

A tear glistened in the corner of her eye. Something about her sadness tore at his heart. She'd been so sunny, so bright, so full of spunk earlier. And now she was steeped in shame because of what he'd just told her. When it had been no fault of hers.

He would have given anything to soften the blow, but now it was done and at least she would be safe from London's most infamous cad.

Before he could say a word to assuage her feelings, they were accosted by her friends.

"Come quickly, Rue! Hurry! Thorndike woke and is mad as a hornet!"

Rusilla Charkova cast him a look that was filled with gratitude. Or regret. He couldn't be sure. But in an instant she disappeared into the crowd with her two girlish companions.

Ned stood on the street corner watching the girls tumble into an open carriage. A distraught older woman stood shaking her finger at them.

It was as it should be, he supposed. But still, it seemed to him that the beautiful girl who'd been thrust in his path twice in less than twenty-four hours had already received her punishment.

He could only wish that Devan Maclyn might receive

punishment as well.

If it were up to him it might well be the fatal kind.

Chapter Four

THERE WAS LITTLE THAT COULD HAVE MADE Ned's day go worse. First he'd had to stay in London a day longer to attend the unveiling of the statue, and then the Charkova girl had managed yet again to get herself into trouble.

But that wasn't the worst of it. Just when he'd planned to return to the country tomorrow, a note arrived from Georgi's mother asking for his indulgence with a last minute escort. It seemed if Gilda couldn't attend Countess Offenbiehl's musicale tonight she would be absolutely devastated.

He was already regretting having agreed to Lord Rathmore's request.

At least the early evening engagement would be short. And completely tame.

They had already arrived in the front hall of the countess's town house, but time seemed to have slowed to a crawl. Ned tugged at his evening waistcoat. His hand reached for his watch fob, but for the hundredth time he resisted checking the hour. Young Gilda most likely wouldn't notice, but he couldn't knowingly be rude to the girl. And where the devil had her mother disappeared to? She'd shot off the moment they came in from the street.

He looked about but was unable to see the errant mother. He was about to voice his displeasure, but thought better of it. Sweet little Gilda was probably as miffed as he was that her father had arranged for a stodgy old duke to squire her about town in his absence. In truth, he usually didn't mind the countess's musicales, but looking after a fourteen-year-old who hadn't yet lost her baby plump had certainly put a damper on the evening.

"May we please sit close to the front?"

Ned looked about and spied three unoccupied chairs in the third row. It was far too close to the front. No discreet escape route. But he would humor the little lass.

"As you wish, Lady Gilda," he smiled. Truthfully, she wasn't a completely unlikable child. She seemed to know her place, had impeccable manners—for a child—and made quite a lovely picture in her evening gown. The frock was clearly new, or at least new to her. Ned could tell because she'd slyly checked herself in every mirror along the way from the countess's front hall to the music room.

As they slipped into the third row, Lady Gilda could scarcely contain her excitement. The moment she sat, she whipped open her Bohemian lace fan and made an admirable effort to banish the flush from her cheeks.

Before he was forced into conjuring up conversation, Lady Rathmore slipped into her chair, and Countess Offenbiehl appeared near the clavichord to begin her welcome. In moments, the music began, and Ned felt its calming influence. Lady Gilda could not have been a more perfect audience. She applauded demurely in all the right places, her pretty fan dangling from her wrist, just like the grand dames seated all around her. Her father could be proud.

After a pleasant hour, Ned settled himself for the final piece, usually the golden jewel of the countess's renowned events. She always saved a lively, sparkling, or dramatic presentation by a well-known musician for the crowning moment of the recital. It was her wish, she often said, to send her patrons out into the world on a joyous note.

Lady Gilda leaned a bit toward him and whispered. "I've heard the last number is going to be spectacular."

Ned smiled at her eagerness. "It usually is, Lady Gilda." He winked. "If you like the final artist, I shall make sure to gain an introduction for you. Would you like that?"

"Oh, Your Grace! How marvelous! Oh my!"

They both shushed themselves, realizing they'd whispered right through the introduction, and turned to see the final artist take her place. The young woman carried an instrument he'd not seen before at close range, but he recognized it immediately. The three-stringed balalaika in the girl's graceful hands was burnished to a beautiful sheen, its contrasting inlaid woods reflecting the light from the chandelier beneath which she was taking her seat.

The artist was dressed in a brightly colored folk costume whose hem scandalously revealed her slim ankles. An intricately wrapped turban of a rich wine color flecked with gold swathed her head, and beneath it tumbled a riot of auburn curls.

With a graceful flourish, the girl tossed a brightly colored fringed fabric over the back of the chair. It fell nicely across the chair, its ends pooling on the floor. It was the perfect throne for the girl who seemed to have walked right out of a portrait.

But if the trappings were strange, her face was not. As she turned to seat herself, her lovely face came fully into view.

Rusilla Charkova.

She crossed her pretty ankles and shifted to position the instrument on her lap. The movement drew Ned's eyes to her lovely small breasts that bubbled with maddening enticement above the bits of lace that formed her décolletage.

Something within Ned's chest expanded into a startled tumble. He'd been taken by her eyes when he danced with her, drawn by her smile when he dragged her from Parliament Square, but none of those reactions compared remotely to what he was feeling now. With her eyes lit in anticipation of her performance and her unexpected bosom revealed, she was positively glorious. He swallowed hard.

And as he drew a calming breath, she positioned herself and spoke.

"Iss no song in whole world more beautiful than song of Ruska Roma."

She struck the strings once, sending the instrument's bright harmonies into the room.

"Iss what you call Russian Gypsy melody."

She struck an ascending chord and let it suspend for a moment.

"It name mean *My Longing Heart.*"

A quieter chord issued from beneath her fingers, and as it hung in the air, her eyes closed once, twice, and then the magic began.

To say that her music charmed him would be an understatement of the first order. With each note and each escalation of the tempo, Ned's body rhythm slid further and further in tandem with the music. He was drawn in and plundered, as if she plucked some magic from the strings that bound his soul to the singer.

As though she sat within the mesmerizing sound itself, Rusilla Charkova swayed back and forth, stretched her neck this way and that, and let her whole body join with the melody. And yet, as she seemed to dance, she never left the chair. Her ankles remained demurely crossed. Only her bosom rose and fell in unity with the music.

Each time her fingers raced to a dramatic pitch signaling the finale, she dove again into the song, making Ned think that she, too, did not want the song to end.

Ned's mood lightened with the rapid high staccatos, and mellowed when the music dipped into melancholy plains. He felt smiles drawn to his face even while sympathy tugged at his heart. Such was the emotion she was able to infuse into her music.

When at last she struck the final chord, her head slowly bowed. At the same time, her hand continued in its natural arc, as if she felt a need to follow the triumphant note out into the universe.

Ned held his breath. Nothing had ever stirred him like the performance he'd just witnessed.

Gilda sat beside him, both hands clasped beneath her chin, her eyes glazed in awe.

No sound was heard in the room until Miss Charkova finally dropped her hand to the instrument, looked up, and cast a beatific smile over her audience. Clearly, she had just returned from some unknowable place.

Ned stood, obeying his need to honor her performance in the only way he could.

"Brava!"

He spoke in a hushed tone. But as the word slipped from his mouth, it seemed to burst his momentary thrall. Reality began to filter in. Had everyone seen him transported? Had he made a fool of himself?

Embarrassment shinnied down his spine. At the same time heat crept up his cheeks.

If he had made a spectacle, it would be the talk of the *ton*.

But they were still focused on the girl's performance. All around him voices broke into high compliments and the applause was slow to die.

In his embarrassment, Ned thrust his elbow toward young Lady Gilda to take his arm. "Come. We're leaving."

"But...but...you promised!" She turned to Lady Rathmore. "Mother? May we stay please? Please?"

"I promised to bring you here and I've done so. Now we're leaving."

"No!" She shrank away. "You promised I could meet her."

"Another time. I'll retrieve your cloak. Follow me."

With that he turned and cleared a path to exit the music room. The sniffling he heard from behind him fueled his embarrassment even further.

Yes, he'd promised the girl she could meet the final artist. But that was before he knew that artist would be Rusilla Charkova.

There was no way in heaven or hell he could be in the presence of that girl. Not after the state her music had put him in. Not after the way her bold gypsy costume and all it revealed had claimed his attention.

Ned tried to be gentle as he thrust Lady Gilda's cloak around her shoulders.

He jammed his top hat on his head and thrust his hands into his gloves. Surely as soon as he could get out into the street that damnable music would stop coursing through his veins.

Surely.

He turned to hand the young lady into the carriage and was thoroughly chastised by the sad look on her face. So chastised, that he swept off his hat, tugged off his white gloves, and threw them with a bit greater force than necessary into his hat. They were going to have to go back inside because the girl's mother had done it yet again.

He let a long sigh trail into the night.

Where the devil had that woman disappeared to this time?

~~~

"Your performance was terribly...athletic, I must say."

A woman who had introduced herself as the dowager duchess of something or other passed her veiled criticism of Rue's performance, even as she patted Rue's hand and smiled.

These Londoners certainly phrased things oddly, but Rue had little doubt that it was masked disapproval the woman was voicing.

She cast a quick look about and reassured herself that appreciation seemed to be the most prevalent reaction. It certainly wasn't disapproval she'd seen on Ned Danton's face. She'd almost bungled the fast arpeggios leading into the finale when she had momentarily glimpsed him just three rows back in the audience. He seemed to be with her note for note as she ascended the music's tantalizing heights.

Rue cast her eyes about the room, but there was no sign of him. He'd been with some woman who Rue had not been able to see, hidden as she was behind a large fellow in the second row. But Ned had been attentive to the female as she waved her pretty fan about. Obviously the woman was more interesting to him than Rue's music, because he hadn't even bothered to stay long enough to greet her.

And she did so wish he had. She had spent the afternoon forming the perfect apology, one that expressed her appreciation for the concern he had shown at the statue unveiling and at the same time rather pointedly indicated he might keep future interventions to himself.

Was that too much to ask?

It was so annoying that now, when the words were still fresh in her mind, she did not have the opportunity to deliver them.

But deliver them she would.

If ever she saw Ned Danton again.

"Well, if it isn't our little gypsy."

Rue turned at the voice and nearly bumped shoulders with Devan Maclyn. How did he have the indecency to greet her? The thought forced an insincere smile to her face.

"My lord, I not real gypsy."

He reached a brazen hand to flick the ruffle of her costume. "You certainly look like one."

He took her by the elbow and steered her into the alcove behind a mammoth Italian screen where she had waited with the other artists for her turn to perform.

His voice was warm and disturbingly thrilling as he recounted the many ways she had moved him with her song. But the moment they were hidden by the screen, his voice changed, suddenly colored with a sensual note. It flustered her, and at the same time brought tingles of pleasant awareness.

Maclyn leaned scandalously close. "You should be more careful of your repertoire, Miss Charkova."

Rather than crane her neck upward to respond, she stepped back daintily. "Vat you mean?"

"You know what I mean," he grinned, and suddenly he was close again. Too close.

"Iss old Russian music. Everyone sing it in my country."

Now she was feeling defensive. She began to turn to the side to make her escape, but he raised his hands to grasp her upper arms. At the same time, he forced her to back up another step, and with alarm she realized she was now cornered. Behind her was the wall, to her left was the tall Italian screen, and before her loomed a man with lust in his eyes.

"Don't play the innocent with me, my little Russian dollie." Now his jaw clenched in a way that heightened her alarm. "Give us a kiss."

He began to lower his head and without even thinking what she was doing, Rue pushed hard on his chest with both her hands. But he was quick, and now he had both her wrists caught painfully in his fists.

"Careful, gypsy whore." He pinned her hands to the wall behind her. "You invited this."

Whore!

The word shocked her beyond belief. She knew its meaning, and having it used on her was an affront like no other she could fathom. He was a brute, a cad, an unscrupulous beast. Just like Ned Danton had said.

Rue began to tell him so, but he crushed her against the wall and blocked her words with his mouth. Before he could manage a kiss, she stomped hard on his foot.

"Why you—"

But it was her turn to block his words, and she put her whole body into the slap she planted on his jaw.

"Never touch me. You hear this?" She heard the threat in her own voice and was satisfied when he stepped away.

She turned an angry shoulder to brush past him, but his bruising fingers caught her hard at the elbow.

"You know you don't mean that."

He crushed his bruising lips against her mouth. But just as she raised her fist to pound his chest, he flew backward, rebounding hard against the wall and knocking over the Italian screen as he fell to the floor.

Beyond the fracas, half the guests were still milling about, and conversation stopped abruptly as the ugly scene was revealed to them. Maclyn lay sprawled on the toppled screen, rubbing his jaw. Rue stood with both hands covering her scream, her turban knocked askew and hair tumbled about her shoulders.

And in front of a cowering Lady Gilda stood the man whose fist had cut short Devan Maclyn's obscene intentions. The anger had not yet left his face, but even so he was the most welcome sight she could have hoped for. She reached a hand to steady herself, but it was not enough. With a startled gasp, she collapsed.

The last thing she was aware of as blackness overtook her was being swept off her feet and into the strong arms of her self-appointed hero. The dashing Duke of Wellbury.

CHAPTER FIVE

"Tsk, tsk."

In the quiet of Katerina Vladimirovna Charkova's private room, Rue's mother clucked her tongue in disapproval.

"You should not think to play gypsy girl with these people. Especially these English men."

Rue looked woefully at her mother. Perhaps it had been a mistake to relate last night's ugly experience while her mother still lay in her bed at *Rosehaven*. Did she really think it was her daughter's performance that had seduced the words from the unscrupulous cad Devan Maclyn? Rue felt the need to protest.

But a long look at her mother's pale face staid her tongue.

"I not do this more times, *mamochka*."

Her mother reached a trembling hand to cradle Rue's cheek. She was so weak! Rue was about to question her mother when she heard the footfall of someone approaching her mother's bed.

She looked up into the bespectacled face of a middle-aged doctor. At least, he wore the white coat of a doctor. To her surprise, when he spoke she heard the comforting hint of a Russian dialect.

"Madame Charkova, what good fortune! Am I at last to meet the daughter of General Charkov?"

The ease with which the man greeted her mother flooded Rue with comfort. She hadn't realized the small tension she'd been living with every day as a foreigner in this city. In truth, it was the small things that surprised her most. Little things, like the fact that these Londoners had no idea there were two forms of her name—one for her father, Charkov, and a feminine form for herself and her mother, Charkova. Was that so difficult to understand? This English culture had no such distinction which completely defied common sense, as far as Rue was concerned.

As Rue recovered from her shock at meeting a compatriot, her mother made the introduction.

"Yevgeny Kablukov, meet my daughter Rusilla Ivanovna Charkova." Her mother turned to her with a sweet smile. "She come to me every day."

"Greetings, Rusilla Ivanovna Charkova." Mr. Kablukov extended his hand as he spoke, and Rusilla offered her own. With a great show of chivalry, the doctor bent halfway to her hand and clicked his heels together with a smart snap.

"It is a great honor to meet the daughter of one who wore the colors of my homeland."

Rue raised her eyebrows in surprise. "You home iss Ukraine?"

He laughed. "Thirty years ago, yes. Odessa. Pearl of the Black Sea."

An overwhelming sense of safety swept over her just hearing this man speak. His manner was as comforting as his voice, and for twenty more minutes the three carried on an engaging conversation. But when Rue's mother tired, they both bade her pleasant dreams and tiptoed away.

"I will take the best possible care of your dear mother, Miss Charkova." He patted her hand. "You go and have a good time. Taste everything London has to offer. I'll look after Katka."

Rue was quite taken aback that he had called her mother by the version of her name used only to show an intimate affection. But perhaps being her only contact within the confines of *Rosehaven Sanatorium*—and being compatriots—had led to an unusual familiarity between the two.

"She mean everything to me," Rue whispered. A tear escaped her eye, and she reached a hand to wipe it away. But not before he gave her free hand a reassuring squeeze.

"She will recover, *zaychik*. I promise."

A wave of melancholy swamped her at his use of the fatherly endearment.

Little rabbit.

Rue managed a smile before she turned to leave. She would allow him his lapses in Russian propriety. Somehow it made it easier to leave than it had been on previous days, knowing her mother was in the care of this kind man.

Even though concern for her mother threatened to ruin her afternoon, she would not let it. After all, she had much for which to be thankful.

Her mother was recovering.

~~~

By mid-afternoon on the day following the musicale, Ned had come to realize that life as he knew it no longer existed. Even as he had escorted Lady Gilda and her mother through the charming grounds of *Vauxhall Gardens* at midday, he could not manage to dispel the tantalizing image of Miss Rusilla Charkova. Or the feel of her in his arms.

Now on his way home after depositing the women at Rathmore House, Ned wiped the perspiration from his brow. The maddening Russian girl who simply couldn't keep herself out of trouble had overtaken his brain for the bulk of the day, and he begged for a diversion from it. If he wasn't mooning over her remarkable eyes or recalling her completely enchanting music, he was swept away into thoughts of what those gifted fingers might do if she were to put down that balalaika.

It was pathetic. *He* was pathetic.

As if things hadn't been bad enough, after the skirmish with Maclyn she had fainted in his arms. Without thinking, Ned had carried Miss Charkova around the fallen screen to seek assistance. At that very moment she roused, tightened her arms about his neck, and planted a grateful kiss on his cheek. He could not have been more aware of it had she branded his cheek with fire. All he had to do was recall the moment and his cheek flamed again. Even now, a full day later.

Ned tried to shake off the disturbing line of thought, but nothing in the busy streets of Mayfair managed to disengage his mind from the brief few moments he'd experienced with Miss Charkova. He felt too alive to simply sit at home, and contemplated telling his driver to drop him at White's—do a bit of gambling to divert his thoughts.

This restlessness he felt was new to him. He realized that in all the years he'd known Georgiana, he'd never had this kind of compulsion to seek her out. Over time, she had become a fixture in his plans for the future. Yet, long weeks would go by between social engagements. And while he was always happy to see her and thoroughly enjoyed their times together, he'd never felt an urgent need to be with her every moment. Humiliating as it was, he began to realize that it had been the same for her.

But it was not so with Miss Rusilla Ivanovna Charkova.

He'd learned a great deal about her in the brief time they'd had to converse as she recovered from Maclyn's assault. She had rested on a chaise in one of Countess Offenbiehl's private drawing rooms and allowed the aging countess to talk her through the trauma. He hadn't intended to stay with the two, but the moment Miss Charkova began to speak, he found himself tethered to the floor. Whether from relief or her natural disposition, nervous chatter spilled from her, giving shape to his first impressions of the young woman. She loved her mother, feared for her mother's health, and visited her sickbed at *Rosehaven* every day. She still mourned her father who evidently had been a revered Russian general. She was treated kindly by her British host families and loved their daughters, Hari and Del. And she loved nothing in the world more than dancing. And perhaps English hot chocolate.

"Next time I run like wind," she had said. "Only not in this shoe." She fussed with her gypsy skirt that left an enticing length of ankle open to view.

Ned had been forced to divert his eyes from staring at the slim ankles that extended beyond the ruffles of her colorful costume.

"Shoes not good for to run," Miss Charkova pouted. "Naked feet iss better."

Heat had crept up the back of Ned's neck. Countess Offenbiehl had merely straightened and covered her surprised chuckle with the back of her ringed fingers.

Naked feet, indeed.

This girl would be the death of him. He was certain of it now. And yet it surprised him that suddenly he wanted her to know his country as he knew it, the England he loved. He would get her out of London to see the countryside, enjoy idyllic days in a sprawling manor house. Dance to her heart's content. And let her naked feet run where they willed.

The carriage slowed and he prepared to step down as it rolled to a stop in the mews. He called to his coachman that he'd be going out again within the hour. Ned swept off his hat, tossed his gloves inside it, and strode toward the rear entrance of Wellbury Place. He was about to take the two steps up to the door when a voice from a shadowed corner halted him.

"Danton!"

The voice was coarse, sandy. *American.*

Ned turned toward the shadows.

"Rockefeller?"

The man who stumbled out of the dimness looked like the wrath of God had descended upon him. His clothes were crude and fit poorly, his face unshaven, and his hands trembled as they held his hat.

"My god, man, what's happened? I thought you'd be in Egypt by now. What's—"

"We were attacked, Your Grace. Didn't even make it to Le Havre. We were at anchor about a hundred yards offshore."

"Attacked!"

"They cast me over the side, but I wasn't badly hurt. I swam around the hull and pulled myself in through the port side loading bay they had lowered to take on supplies. I managed to get Georgi into the water and strapped her to a bale of cork and swam to shore, pulling her.

"Is...is she alright?"

Solomon Rockefeller looked at Ned with pain in his eyes. "Her father was killed by the marauders. They knew what they were after. And Georgiana—"

"What about her? Out with it!"

Rockefeller dropped his voice to a whisper. "She's very badly hurt. She's been in and out of consciousness for most of five days now."

Ned raked a hand through his hair, trying to make sense of it all. He put a hand on Solomon Rockefeller's shoulder and steered him toward the door. "Come in, come in. This is dreadful."

He hurried the man toward his study and poured two glasses of brandy.

"Is she in hospital?"

Rockefeller shook his head. "We didn't dare." He gulped at his brandy. "Not safe. First place they'd look."

"Well then, where did you take her?"

"She's in a room over the Trade Winds Taproom below Canary Wharf. I thought she was going to be alright, but she's getting worse. I need to move her to something...someplace where a decent doctor can tend her." He emptied his glass. "It's bad, Danton. Real bad." He shook his head. "They knew we were coming."

"Wait. Who? Who knew you were coming."

"The attackers. They were English. They knew what we were carrying and they didn't care who they killed to get it."

Ned took a shaky breath as he replenished the man's brandy.

"What were you carrying?"

Rockefeller let out a long, weary sigh. "All of our expeditionary and archeological excavation equipment, of course. And..."

Ned watched him wrestle with the rest of what he needed to say.

"And?" Ned prodded.

Rockefeller looked at the floor for a long minute, then finally raised his eyes and spoke in a hushed tone.

"We had the *Stones of Saqqarah*—the last of the missing jewels from the tomb of the Pharaoh Djoser."

Ned shook his head. "I don't understand. You hadn't excavated yet. How could you—"

Rockefeller shoved his hands into his pockets. "They were stolen from Djoser's tomb centuries ago. Lord Rathmore managed to buy them on the black market. He's been collecting them for years. It took nearly every penny he had but he finally had them all. That's the only reason he took me along, because I helped him locate some of the gems. We were taking them back where they belonged. Sort of extra incentive for the Pasha to provide permissions and security for our new excavations."

"Georgiana's father died returning a national treasure?"

"Lost his fortune and his life. And the jewels."

Ned could only stand in shock.

"How could they possibly be worth that kind of risk, Solomon? I don't understand."

Rockefeller huffed out a despairing laugh.

"It was a valuable cache, Your Grace. Several antiquities, six enormous diamonds, and the two great emeralds from Djoser's eyes. It was Rathmore's dream to restore them to their rightful home." Rockefeller swept a hand through his greasy hair. "His name would have gone down in history as the man who found the *Stones of Saqqarah*. And Georgi's, too."

"And your own," Ned said quietly. "To say nothing of the reward, which would have been mammoth, I should think."

Rockefeller darted him a look that at first seemed sad, then pained. "It will mean nothing to me if Georgi dies." He stopped pacing and stood before Ned. "You have to help me, Your Grace. If anything happens to her I—"

Ned put a hand on Solomon's shoulder. The man was clearly in love with Georgi. He'd been a fool not to see it before. And now Georgi's fixation with the man made all the more sense.

"What can I do?"

Solomon heaved a great sigh, as if he'd dared not hope Ned would be willing. "Help me get her to a doctor, Your Grace. A doctor who can save her. And hide her."

Ned gave Solomon's shoulder a reassuring squeeze. Georgi had been his dearest friend since before he could remember. He'd teased her more times than he dared to admit, and until recent hours had thought her to be the perfect wife for him. But as if the skies had opened and showered him with a dose of reality, Ned knew that Fate had other plans for Georgi, and they didn't include him. Her fate seemed to have bound her to this American adventurer.

"Have another drink while I change into something a bit less, well, less. You stay as you are. I think I know the perfect person to help us out."

With a brisk nod he excused himself and bounded up the stairs two at a time, hastening to change into the leather breeches he wore when he felt like working in the mews. Within seconds he was satisfied he looked like any other stable hand. He grabbed his flop hat and raced to join the American, praying fervently that the person he was certain could help him would do so.

CHAPTER SIX

RUE RAN A CAREFUL FINGER across the finely stitched red shawl. The sweet warmth that washed over her heart took her by surprise. Her rescuer had thrown it across her shoulders to save her modesty yesterday, but it was the way he had fastened it that had her blood racing in her veins.

They'd been standing in front of the vendor's stall, and he was admonishing her to hold it more casually, as if it were a normal thing for her to wear such a wanton red thing in the middle of the day. The handsome duke's chestnut eyes froze her in place as he lifted the fringed ends and secured them in a loose knot across her bosom. As he moved, his fingers brushed her repeatedly, ever so slightly, but with startling effect. Each touch had sent a thrill tumbling to her toes.

"Rue, are you still drooling over that garish thing?" Del scolded as she flounced into the room. "It's scandalously red, I must say, but I suppose it is pretty. In its own way."

Rue drew the shawl around her shoulders and stepped in front of the mirror.

"Look, my Del! It have stars!"

And it did. The way it was draped, a most intricately woven tumble of brightly colored stars straddled her right shoulder. Rue dropped the tails of the shawl into the loose knot Ned had shown her, then turned and twisted to see the subtle decorations that adorned the lush fabric.

"Oh rats, I almost forgot." Del held an envelope out to Rue. "This was just delivered."

Rue took the envelope. The masculine scrawl spelled out her entire name—mostly correctly.

"Well, read it!" Del prompted. "Who is it from? What does it say?"

Rue smiled impishly at her dear friend and minced her way across the room to drop herself onto a chintz boudoir chair. She slid the note from its envelope and held it close, sending a clear message that she wished to read the note in private.

It was brief. Just a few swiftly penned words. As she read, her smile began to slip.

> *My dear young lady,*
> *I am in need of your help on an errand which requires utmost secrecy. If you feel you can trust me, there will be a carriage waiting in front of the bookseller near you on Chancery Lane at half three.*
> *A chaperone will wait at your garden gate to accompany you. If you cannot for any reason join me, I shall understand.*
>
> > *Yours in secrecy,*
> > *Your noble Purveyor of Shawls*

Rue read the note a second time, searching for a sign that this was a bit of mischief. His Grace had chosen not to sign his name. In fact, were the note found lying about, nobody could tell who it was from. Or to whom it was written, for that matter. Even so, the purveyor of shawls left no doubt as to his identity.

Of course she would go. She loved books. Of course she would help him in this matter of great secrecy. She brushed a fallen curl back from her face. Just to be on the safe side, she would tell no one, not even Del.

"Is nice words," she said with a careless, dismissing wave of her hand. But to keep the note from curious eyes, she tucked it into the bodice of her day dress.

"Not fair, Rue. Read it!"

Del stomped her foot playfully.

"Possible later. But you forget time for dancing lesson."

"I—oh, my goodness! You're right!" Del began darting around the room, changing her gown and freshening her hair. "Delfinia Wayburton, when oh when will you get your head on straight." She scolded herself mercilessly for forgetting her lesson as she flew about.

Rue caught hold of Del and posed her before the mirror. "You head look straight to Rue. Now go."

Del gasped, then laughed, then turned and crushed Rue in one of her always-welcome hugs.

"You won't be too bored while I'm gone?"

Board?

Rue smiled. "I not be piece of wood. I read in garden. Now go!" She turned Del toward the door and gave her a small nudge. Why people thought she would turn into a wooden plank every time they left her alone was still mystifying. But she was so grateful for today's fortunate timing. Del's mother would accompany Del to her lesson, then the two would stop at the shops on their way back, as they always did. Rue would have nearly two hours to slip away and meet the duke.

She had no time to waste. The clock on her dressing table already showed ten minutes past three. Rue scooped up a book from the nightstand and made her way to the garden, reminding herself to stop touching the note that was tucked securely inside her chemise. She laid her book on the garden bench before she slipped out through the gate.

A well-dressed woman stepped to her side and smiled, then indicated they should walk together. Though Rue tried her best to quiz her companion, the woman would reveal little. She claimed to be the proprietress of *Barrowburn Book Shoppe*, the one on the lane nearest to Wayburton House.

Within minutes they arrived at the shop. The woman paused in front of the display window and told Rue that His Grace the Duke of Wellbury wished a word. With a nod toward the two-horse cab waiting at the curb, the woman turned away.

Rue gaped at the cab, then turned abruptly toward the book shop window, as if something in there held intense interest for her. And it did. She saw herself reflected there, wearing the gypsy shawl. Her hand flew to her mouth. She'd forgotten she was wearing it when she left the garden. She'd meant to leave it on the bench.

Foolish Rue, she thought. *You want to be invisible, not be wearing this!*

But there was nothing to be done about it now.

She raised her eyes to take in the entire reflection, and realized she had a clear view of the waiting cab. When she had first looked, the interior had seemed dark and empty, the driver disinterested. But now a man's face was visible in the shadows, and a person's hand beckoned to her.

She turned slowly, and when the carriage door swung open, she walked briskly to it and without breaking stride, accepted the hand of the Duke of Wellbury. She smiled at him as she stepped into the carriage.

She slipped past his knee to take the far seat and realized he was not dressed. Not in the way of current fashion, at any rate. His breeches were worn and patched, his shirtsleeves rolled up and grubby, with shredding braces stretched across the work shirt of a common laborer.

"You came," he said.

"Why not I come?"

She allowed him to help her settle into the seat beside him. The opposite seat was occupied by a similarly-dressed fellow who regarded her with wary eyes. Rue clutched her reticule tighter. He in turn clutched a suspiciously human-shaped bundle wrapped in the carriage lap robe.

"Did you tell anyone you were meeting me?"

The duke's voice held an edge of alarm that triggered a worry she'd managed to ignore until now.

"*Nyet*. I tell no one."

"Good. Rusilla Ivanovna Charkova, meet Solomon Rockefeller."

His Grace hurried through the introduction.

The stranger put one finger to the brim of his hat and nodded. "Miss Charkova. We'll be awfully glad if you can help us."

"Miss Charkova—" His Grace swept the hair off his forehead and turned toward her so he could look her straight in the eye.

Rue studied the worry lines that seemed more deeply etched in his forehead today and took pity. Something very troubling had happened. Or was happening. The very least she could do was release him from such formality.

"Please, Your Grace, you to call me Rue."

He let a long breath escape, as if the invitation was a great relief to him.

"And you must call me Ned."

"Friends call me Sol, ma'am."

The man's small smile and slow accent put her at greater ease. Whatever these men wanted, she sensed no danger in it.

"Rue iss happy in help." She smiled at each of the men, and could not miss the look they exchanged. His Grace cleared his throat and shifted slightly.

"We need a doctor, Rue. But no one must know. Our friend is very badly hurt, and some very dangerous men are looking for...for the friend."

He swept a nervous hand down his jawline, and as his worry mounted, Rue resisted a shocking urge to cradle his cheek with her own hand.

"We must act fast but...we can't take the friend to a hospital, or to any doctor who might know me. They'll already be watching those places."

Now her hand reached of its own volition to cover his hand that was fidgeting nervously with his knee.

"You have much big worry, Your Grace. Ned. But I not know how—"

He interrupted her. "I thought of the sanatorium where your mother is. The place you told me about yesterday. Would you be willing—?"

He spoke in a rush, his words tumbling out as fast as a person could speak.

"Oh! Da! Yes, iss doctor there. Yevgeny Kablukov. You want him help you friend?"

"Yes!" Both men responded at the same time, clearly relieved to have the name of a doctor who might help.

"Sanatorium iss name *Rosehaven*. You know it?"

Ned visibly relaxed. "Ah yes. Of course. *Rosehaven*. Thank you, Rue. We'll take our friend there."

He put his hand on the door handle. "I can't thank you enough for coming. I'll let you know—"

Rue reached a hand to stop him from swinging the door wide. "I go with," she said in a tone that she hoped sounded final.

"We can't possibly—"

"I go to see my mother. You take Rue as thank you for favor. Da?"

The duke began to protest but she shushed him. "Put girl in street with no chaperone iss very bad, Your Grace. Crying girl come out of carriage? Tsk tsk. Very bad." She turned a woeful face to him and was pleased to see she had silenced his objections.

He pulled the door closed, and in an instant had called out instructions to the driver, begging him to make all haste. An instant later the carriage joined the stream of traffic making its way down Chancery Lane toward the main thoroughfare.

"May I ask friend name? Who this man who needing help?"

Once again the two men gave each other a questioning look. Seeing agreement, Solomon Rockefeller drew the lap robe away from the bundle that lay against his chest, revealing the face of a woman who had been savagely beaten.

Rue gasped. The woman wore the clothes of a poor tradesman's wife, her hair unkempt. If Rue was not mistaken, those tangled knots were saturated with old blood.

Rue watched as Sol drew his hand lovingly across her swollen cheek, carefully avoiding the most damaged flesh.

"As you can see, it's not a man who needs our help, Rue," Ned said quietly. "It's her. Lady Georgiana Rathmore."

Rue gasped. This was the lovely girl who danced so prettily at the ball, but the young woman who lay in Solomon Rockefeller's arms was unrecognizable.

As she stared at the poor thing's injuries she could barely whisper. This was the friend who needed her help. This was the friend these men were begging her to rescue. To hide.

Lady Georgiana Rathmore.

The Duke of Wellbury's sweetheart.

~~~

"You say the woman's husband did this?"

Rue nodded, keeping to the story they'd contrived before reaching *Rosehaven Sanatorium*.

"She iss sister of my maid. Please, you to help? I pay you well."

They had been so lucky to find Dr. Kublakov in Rue's mother's private hospital room. His Grace had insisted Rue take the lead while he and Rockefeller merely acted as laborers carrying the poor woman on a stretcher. From the looks he was getting, Ned Danton had the staff thoroughly confused. Rugged as he looked in his rough clothing, his regal bearing was a complete giveaway. It was true he had the muscles one would expect to find on a peasant. Rue had spent a long moment appreciating that very fact. But anyone looking twice would surely suspect his pedigree.

Solomon wasn't doing too well, either. His concern for Georgiana, touching her hand, wiping a tear from his eye, clearly revealed that the unconscious woman was more to him than they had admitted. Rue was most curious how Ned Danton was handling the fact that Solomon held such obvious affection for Lady Georgiana. Furtive looks at the duke gave her no answer in that regard.

As the minutes passed, the two men managed to avoid scrutiny. All eyes were focused on the brutally injured unconscious young woman.

It had taken all of Rue's cleverness to be vague while answering Kablukov's questions. She had sworn him to secrecy in Russian before explaining her need for a private bed for her mystery patient. The woman was, she insisted, in mortal danger from the man who had beaten her senseless a week earlier. For that reason they would refer to her as Mrs. Talbott, to protect her if the husband came looking for her. Beyond that, Rue remained almost ridiculously hazy.

Rue stood at the foot of the hospital bed and forced herself to be clear-headed about the story they'd agreed upon. "Y-yes. Eliza Talbott husband iss brute. Very bad man. I must know, Yevgeny Kablukov, she will live?"

She looked with worry on the scene before her. Poor Lady Georgiana seemed to be barely breathing. Even now that the nurse had cleaned her wounds and the worst of them were being stitched up, she looked as if life was slowly taking its leave.

"I'll know more tomorrow, my dear. In the meantime, I shall keep her close, right by my office. The poor woman has been unconscious far too long. All I can say is, be prepared for the worst. It's such a shame you didn't bring her in sooner."

"I...yes...we must to go now." She stepped closer to the doctor. "*Pomni svoye obeshchaniye.*"

"I promise, my dear. No one will know your friend is here."

He patted her hand and gave her a reassuring smile.

"Your secret is safe with me."

~~~

Ned stepped out of the carriage to deliver Rue to her host family's town house. He was completely taken with her skill at subterfuge, her ability to keep the story just vague enough to ward off questions. What young woman could have handled today's crisis with the aplomb she had displayed?

He turned to help her alight from the carriage step. Her striking red shawl fluttered about her, adding a grace that the girl simply didn't need. She had every feminine grace a girl's mother could hope for.

"I go to garden first. They think I be there all this time." She bobbed a curtsy and began to turn but Ned did not release her hand.

"No, Rue. I'll tell them you were with me. That they must forgive your transgression because I required your assistance. Come."

He gave her hand a tug and drew her with him up the steps and into the house.

"Tell Lady Wayburton we wish to see her," he instructed the

startled butler.

"Duke of Wellbury," Ned prompted. "Forgive my dress."

The butler looked abashed at not having recognized him, and disappeared in a hurry.

"Your Grace, iss no need. I am fine to go to garden. They find me there. They never know what we do."

He smiled at her sudden girlish fears. After the maturity she had shown in pulling off the deception at the hospital, he was rather pleased to see her innocence rise again to the surface.

"Rusilla! Wherever have you been?"

Lady Wayburton swept into the foyer, all motherly concern that turned to disapproval the moment she saw who was with her young house guest. Until she recognized him, that is.

"Your...Your Grace?"

Ned forestalled her questions.

"Lady Wayburton, you are too kind to receive us. I wonder if we may speak in private?"

Ned took charge of the conversation, giving instructions intended to cut short the interrogation he could see was on the tip of her tongue.

"Of course, Your Grace." She turned to the butler. "See that tea is brought to the drawing room, Philbert."

She turned with a rather stiff nod and led the way across the hall.

Ned wasted no time getting to the point.

"Lady Wayburton, you should know that Miss Charkova has been of invaluable service to the Crown today."

It wasn't really an exaggeration. Lord Rathmore had been a favorite of the Queen, after all. It was the Queen who had begged Rathmore to undertake the voyage to return the jewels to the government of Egypt in the first place.

"She what? Rusilla, whatever does His Grace mean?"

"Unfortunately, she is unable to explain, my lady," he answered for Rue. He turned toward the nervous young lady and captured her eyes. "She has been sworn to a vow of secrecy on the subject. Haven't you, Miss Charkova?"

Rue nodded. But her eyes never strayed from his. In them he felt he could read every question, every emotion, every fear that was churning through her pretty head. And beneath the gentle sweep of her brow he also read her gratitude.

"Until our current diplomatic crisis is resolved, we may need to call upon Miss Charkova further. At any moment. Day or night. For her services as...as a translator." Now he might be exaggerating a bit, but it was the kind of thing Lady Wayburton might be inclined to believe. And the doctor was, after all, Russian.

"I'm certain that will meet with your approval?" Ned turned a deferential eye toward the somewhat befuddled woman. "Her mother has, of course, given her daughter full permission to participate in this...matter of great national import." That was the truth. Or nearly.

His words flustered the poor woman. Lady Wayburton sputtered a bit as she fanned herself rather furiously until at last she stood.

"Your Grace, Miss Charkova will make herself available to you at any time you require her presence. You have only to ask. On one condition."

"Anything, my lady."

"You will vouch for her safety, Your Grace. In fact, you shall never, not for a moment, let her out of your sight when on one of your...missions."

Ned smiled and turned toward Rue. "I promise to protect her with my very life." He angled his body just enough to conceal the fact that he drew a small 'X' over his heart. Rue's answering blush drew a smile from him that threatened to turn into a laugh.

"And now I bid you all good day."

Ned gave a courtly bow and turned on his heel to make his escape before Rue's host might think to question him further. Why the devil had he done that? What he truly meant to promise was that he would never again, under any circumstances, draw this lovely young woman into anything even remotely risky.

She was, he suddenly realized, far, far too precious.

CHAPTER SEVEN

RUE COULD SCARCELY CONTAIN HER JOY.

She had spent the night visited by the sweetest of dreams and now fairly floated through the morning. Another pretty tussie mussie nosegay from Ned had arrived. He was literally showering her with gestures of thanks. The flowers sat in a jeweled vase on her lamp table, their fragrance wafting promises of something she didn't quite dare let herself contemplate. The duke was, after all, in love with another woman—one who at this moment seemed barely clinging to life.

But within the small nosegay the duke had tucked a note expressing his fervent—oh, what a pretty word—his fervent hope that she would save a waltz on her dance card at tonight's ball. Could it be his heart was not yet promised? The prospect practically set her feet to dancing.

And just moments ago, in the midst of it all, she had received the best possible news from her mother's doctor—news which sent her off two hours early for what would be her last daily visit to *Rosehaven*.

She'd been thrilled to find her mother no longer in bed, but sitting prettily in the side chair, dressed to the height of fashion.

"You to come home? Oh *mamochka*! Iss wonderful!"

Rue clasped her mother's hand and kissed it.

"She must stay confined to bed for two more weeks, my dear," Yevgeny Kablukov warned with a smile, "but she is prepared to go with you today."

The doctor took his patient's hand. "The sooner you regain your strength, the sooner I can show you all the London sights we spoke of."

The look he exchanged with her mother startled Rue. A heat seemed to simmer between them, an ardor that had not been present on previous visits.

He reached a hand to touch Katerina Charkova's cheek. "I shall call on you tomorrow at your residence, Katka."

Rue's eyebrows lifted even further in surprise. There it was again—the intimate exchange.

The glorious smile her mother gave the man left little room for doubt. Their fondness for one another was growing stronger by the day.

"Tomorrow, Yevgenyevich Kablukov."

Her mother's use of the affectionate form of the doctor's given name—changing Yevgeny to Yevgenyevich—convinced her she was right. Rue wasn't sure how she felt about that. All the tender touching, the smouldering looks, and now the intimate nicknames told a story she felt quite sure she didn't want to hear. Not at the moment, anyway.

Katka? Yevgenyevich? Really? Those were for a husband and wife to use. Or lovers.

She could not help watching her mother's eyes as they followed the doctor's progress out of the private room. She would take her mother home today, but her intuition told her there was no doubt she would be seeing the good doctor again.

Rue smiled. She had come on her visit today thinking she would tell her mother all about the Duke of Wellbury and the hopes that had suddenly sprung in her heart. But that would keep. When she shared it with her mother, she wanted her mother's full attention.

Today that clearly was not going to happen.

~~~

Halfway down the hallway beyond the women's ward, another visitor stepped out of a darkened alcove as Kablukov drew close to his office. The doctor's eyes widened in anticipation.

"Do you have them?"

Kablukov checked the hallway in both directions and quickly drew Devan Maclyn into his office.

Maclyn dropped into a chair and threw his hat to the floor. "No, I bloody hell do not have them. Do you think I'd be here if I did?"

The doctor fumed a bit, clenching his hands into fists.

"What. Went. Wrong."

"Look, don't blame me. We did everything you said." Maclyn angrily swept an imaginary bit of dust from his knee. "My men were dressed just like you told me. And there were no witnesses. None. If there had been, all they would have seen was a pack of dirty Bedouins sacking the ship."

Kablukov seethed.

"Tell me what happened. And don't leave anything out."

With a begrudging shrug, the usually defiant young man

drew a long breath. "Our bunch boarded the ship and took the party captive. Just off Le Havre, like you said to. They searched every inch of the boat. Every box, every satchel. Even stripped the party naked." He shook his head. "All we got was a small crate of minor stones. The two giant emeralds and the six big diamonds just weren't there, Kablukov. I dunno. Maybe my informant got it wrong."

Kablukov slammed a fist on his desk. "Rathmore had the jewels, alright, you halfwit. I managed to confirm that. But you..." He pointed a shaky finger at Maclyn. "...you couldn't find them?"

"I wasn't there. I couldn't—" Maclyn drew his hands through his hair in frustration. "Rathmore and his daughter know me. I couldn't go on the boat. You know that!"

With an angry sweep of his hand, Kablukov knocked the books off his desktop. "Idiot! My god, boy, you were going to kill them anyway! Who cares if they recognized you?" He pounded the desk again. "Imbecile!"

Kablukov collapsed into the chair behind his desk.

Devan Maclyn muttered a word of apology and rose to leave.

"Sit down," Kablukov commanded.

Maclyn turned.

"What for? It's over."

Kablukov slowly shook his head.

"We were so close." He took in a long breath. "Tell me what you did with the bodies."

Maclyn reached to the floor and recovered his hat. He swallowed hard.

"They were thrown overboard."

Kablukov nodded. "All of them?"

Maclyn stood scuffing his booted toe against the floor.

"Son?"

"They left the girl. She looked dead but they were superstitious about throwing her overboard."

"Bloody hell. What did they do with the body once they were in port?"

"They didn't."

Kablukov sat up. "What the hell do you mean, they didn't?"

Maclyn looked up. "I mean that they had to tidy up and change clothes before they could sail on to Gibraltar to dispose of the ship. And when they went to get the body she—"

"She what?"

Maclyn swallowed hard.

"She was gone."

~~~

Rue helped her mother into a wheeled chair the nurse had provided, relieved to be taking her home.

"Oh, Mama. You beautiful."

"And you, daughter, you as well." She reached out to finger the red shawl Rue had taken to wearing as often as possible. "But this..." she sighed. "What are we to do with this, eh?"

Rue laughed. Her mother couldn't be expected to understand what the red shawl meant to her. Perhaps one day she'd be able to explain. Rue took a position behind her mother's chair and wheeled it out of the private room and into the corridor. But instead of turning toward the front door, she turned toward the ward where Lady Georgiana lay.

"Iss someone I show you," Rue whispered after dismissing

the nurse. "She iss Duke of Wellbury sweetheart. No say this to anyone, but I help bring sweetheart here. She in much danger so here she hide. We just go to say goodbye. But Mama, she hurt bad, sleep only."

Rue propped aside the curtain that shielded Lady Georgiana from the rest of the ward and wheeled her mother to the woman's bedside. She misjudged the confined space and bumped one wheel of the chair against the bed.

Georgiana moaned.

The sound startled Rue. In the time she'd been stopping to check on Lady Georgiana, the woman had never made so much as a peep. Perhaps this was a good sign?

Once her mother was situated, Rue slipped around to the opposite side of the bed and took Lady Georgiana's hand. "I bring my mama today, my lady." Rue caressed the sleeping young woman's hand as she had so many times. "Solomon to come, sit with you tonight. He sad you not talk him."

She continued to croon softly, moving her hands gently up and down along her ladyship's arms. It was more than she'd ventured before, but it seemed to be getting a response.

"*Mamochka*, look! She move!"

Rue cradled Lady Georgiana's cheeks and gently rocked them back and forth, moving the woman's head as carefully as she could.

All of the sudden, the woman snapped her head in the opposite direction.

"No!"

The woman cried softly, making Rue fear she might have been too rough with the patient.

"No," the lady whimpered again.

The woman's head moving from side to side on the pillow dislodged a pretty band of lace and linen that she had woven through her unkempt curls. With great care, Rue lifted it from her head, thinking she would reseat the ribboned band, or lay it on the bedside table.

But Lady Georgiana's hand whipped upward to grab her wrist. "No!" she cried again.

And this time her eyes flew open.

"Iss me, my lady. Rusilla Ivanovna Charkova." She smiled in an effort to comfort the young woman. "My friend iss Duke of Wellbury," she whispered. "We bring you here. And this my mother." Katerina smiled and nodded on the far side of the bed.

"Neddie? Oh!"

Now Lady Georgiana saw what Rue had in her hand and she gasped. Her eyes flitted back and forth several times, looking first at Rue's hands, then her eyes, then back to her hands. "Hide them," she whispered.

It made no sense to Rue. "What to hide, my lady?"

Lady Georgiana took Rue's hand and closed it over the rose-colored lace and linen band. As she pressed Rue's fingers into the pretty accessory, Rue felt unexpected odd shapes, like rocks, inside the band, where there should be nothing but fabric.

Rue gasped. "This is—?"

Lady Georgiana thrust her shaking hand over Rue's mouth to silence her. "Yes. The *Stones of Saqqarah*," she whispered. "Take them to Solomon and tell him he must not come here!" She was so weak and frightened that her whisper was barely a thread of air escaping from her pale lips. Rue worked hard to hear what she said, because the woman kept looking at the wall that stretched across one side of her curtained cubicle.

Rue shrank back in shock. Was it possible that the jewels everyone thought had gone missing were right here, caught up in this swath of lace? She ran her thumbs across the bumpy folds, and now it made sense. The lines of each buried object were smooth and clean. Lady Georgiana had kept them hidden in plain sight the whole time, as if the lace that concealed them was merely a device to keep her unruly curls in place. Now they clicked softly as Rue nudged them about, like the sound when her fingers rummaged through her jewelry box.

"This I take to Solomon," she whispered.

"Yes! But stay away from the Russian doctor!" Lady Georgiana kept pointing frantically to the wall behind Rue. "He sent my father's killer. And that other man who's with him. I know his voice but I...I just can't place it. He killed them all!"

Tears rushed down her cheeks. She shoved back the covers and struggled to get out of bed, but she became faint again. "We have to get out of here," she whispered in terror.

Rue put out her hands to comfort the distraught young woman.

"It not possible they know you here. Please, my lady. I know this doctor. He make my *mamochka* well. Not to worry! We tell them false name. You not Georgiana. You Mrs. Eliza Talbott."

But the young woman was so distraught now that Rue was concerned Lady Georgiana might do something foolish. She seemed frantic over what she'd heard from the adjoining room. But Rue had heard nothing. It had to have been the young lady's imagination. She had only just awakened. Perhaps disorientation and confusion were to be expected.

Besides, murder? That simply couldn't be.

At that moment a nurse stepped through the curtain. "Mrs. Talbott! You're awake!" As quickly as she appeared, she vanished into the corridor calling for the doctor.

"Hurry! Twist them into your hair! Don't let them know you have them!"

"But I not—"

"Do it! Now!"

Lady Georgiana pushed Rue's hand toward her head, and to keep the lady from becoming more agitated, Rue twisted the heavy dark band with its hidden gems into her own curls.

"I heard them talking. They paid men to attack Father's ship. They—" she choked. "They killed my father."

Her terrified whisper tore at Rue's heart. She looked at her mother who was simply gaping at the two. She hadn't a clue what the connection was between her daughter and this distraught woman.

Before Rue had a chance to explain, the curtain was whisked back and a smiling Doctor Kablukov stepped to the foot of the bed. "Well, now, Mrs. Talbott. You've joined us at last."

He seemed genuinely pleased. But a moment later his face began to change. He looked first at Georgiana, then Rue's mother, then Rue. All three women were turned toward him, their faces etched with fright. It took him only a second to realize what had happened. He looked from them to the wall behind Rue.

"So. You heard."

The women were frozen in silence.

"Damn and blast, you heard it all."

Rue barely dared to breathe. But when Devan Maclyn stepped into the cubicle, her fears and confusion escalated painfully.

Suspicion flooded his face, wiping away any trace of the devilishly handsome young earl.

"What's going on, Kablukov?"

"They heard us. The Russian chit. Her mother. And Mrs. Talbott."

Maclyn looked toward the figure in the bed.

"That," he pointed to Georgiana, "is *not* Mrs. Talbott."

~~~

Ned was more grateful than he could say. He'd been fascinated with the way Rue Charkova had cleverly facilitated Georgiana's care. And she'd done it so easily, slipping into character as if she had been born to the role. In their brief encounters, she had charmed him, enchanted him, and entangled him in a net of her beguilingly garbled English.

He expected she'd gone to *Rosehaven* to see her mother today, and he looked forward to her report. He had no doubt that she'd stop in to check on Georgi as she'd promised.

Ned shuffled the documents that cluttered his desk. There were a thousand things he could have done with his afternoon, but a packet from one of the queen's liveried couriers had tied him to his desk. She'd summoned him to meet with the Home Secretary that very afternoon to finalize his own trip to Egypt. She was sending a most extraordinary group of dignitaries to the opening of the Suez Canal, and Ned had dared not refuse. Perhaps she'd taken a look at the old codgers on the list and decided a younger face or two were in order. Whatever her motivation, acquainting himself with the diplomatic packet had now kept him chained to his desk until it was time to get to

Buckingham Palace to meet with the delegation.

In a selfish move, Ned had taken Rue and the Wayburton women for a drive in the park just that morning. Now her last words to him set his heart scuttling about as if he were a blushing schoolboy.

"Tonight we dance, my Ned."

~~~

Mere hours later, and weary after meticulously following all aspects of court etiquette, Ned put diplomatic matters behind him and began to relax. He was so ready for that dance Rue had promised. In fact, he was actually impatient for it.

Ned cast a glance about the ballroom.

My Ned.

He knew it was just her way of translating her language into his, but it had startled and captivated him. He'd thought of little else since the moment the words had spilled from her lush lips.

He'd dressed for tonight's engagement with great care, for some reason wanting everything to be perfect for her at the Sunderland ball.

Ned spotted Rue's chaperone and moved to greet her, but the woman's worried expression squelched his words.

"What *exactly* are you doing here, Your Grace?"

Ned straightened as he came face to face with a clearly annoyed Lady Wayburton.

"Looking for your house guest actually, my lady."

He gave her a welcoming bow that served to startle her out of her annoyance.

"You mean, she's not with you?"

"And why would she be, my lady?"

"But...well, you said," she began to sputter, "you said you might require her presence at any time. I just assumed—"

"You assumed what, Lady Wayburton?"

Now Ned was becoming unsettled. He didn't at all care for the way his heart had suddenly thudded to a stop.

"I assumed that when she did not return from visiting her mother that you must have waylaid her and trundled her off to some clandestine assignation. At the Queen's behest, of course!"

"Madam, I assure you that should I ever do such a thing it will not be without first sending you a note to that effect. The last I saw Miss Charkova was at your doorstep this morning after our turn in the park."

"But that was hours ago!"

"My lady, when did *you* last see her?"

"Why, just after lunch when she left for *Rosehaven* with Thorndike."

Ned fought his annoyance. "Then Thorndike has not returned, either?"

"Well, of course she has. There was no need of her after Miss Charkova was safely inside the sanatorium."

"You're saying...?"

"No need for a chaperone, my lord, because the girl's mother was coming home with her. Oh dear. This is dreadful. I don't—"

"Not to worry yourself over it, my lady. I'll get it sorted. Now if you will excuse me..."

It was the height of rudeness and he didn't care a whit.

Ned burst through the crowd like an Ascot horse and raced

from the ballroom.

Something was wrong. He knew it in his bones.

Something was terribly wrong.

He became more agitated with each minute as he beat on the roof of his carriage yelling at his coachman to hurry it along.

When at last he reached his town house he raced through the front hall and started up the stairs to change out of his blacks and get his pistol. A noise in his study stopped him.

Was she here?

He turned practically mid-leap and dashed to his study.

"Rue?"

But the moment he stepped in, he knew who had made the noise. And it was not the Russian beauty he'd been hoping to see.

"Sol. What are you doing here?"

"You're out of brandy, Danton."

Ned walked to his desk. "Forget the brandy, Sol. What are you doing here? And where is Rue?"

"Rue? How the devil should I know?"

"She didn't come home from *Rosehaven* this afternoon," Ned said in a rush. "Something's wrong."

He reached into his desk to retrieve his pistol from its case.

"Wait! I'm coming with you." Sol put down the empty brandy decanter and shrugged into his jacket.

At the same time, alarmed voices sounded from the front hall.

Both men sped into the foyer, just in time to see Lady Georgiana collapse on the cold tile.

Still in her hospital gown.

CHAPTER EIGHT

RUE PRAYED FOR A NURSE, an orderly, anyone to interrupt the frightening scene that was unfolding at Lady Georgiana's bedside.

"We'll take these two to the cellar and come back for Rathmore's daughter."

Rue felt Maclyn's rough hand grip her arm.

"You not hurt my mother," she cried. "She very sick!"

Rue was stunned. These men she thought she knew had suddenly turned into brutes.

Kablukov leaned down to speak in her mother's ear.

"I wish you hadn't heard all this, Katka. I really do. But I can explain—"

"Then let Rusilla go. She knows nothing to hurt you." Rue's mother turned her face up to smile sweetly at Kablukov. "I myself will go with you, my Yevgenyevich."

Rue heard the false note in her mother's voice and wondered at her coolness in the situation that only moments ago had turned so frightening. Taking courage from her, Rue seized the opportunity to kick at a small wash stand and send its metal pan clattering to the floor. The racket seemed to echo forever in the small, empty ward, but nobody came to investigate.

With a sharp command, the two men dragged the women from the bedside and hurried them along the private end of the corridor. The doctor opened a large cupboard door, pulled her mother from the wheeled chair, and shoved her to the cupboard floor.

"Vat you do? Stop!"

Maclyn slapped Rue. Hard.

"Quiet, or I'll do the same to your mama."

Rue shrank from his cruelty and turned away, just in time to see her mother disappear beyond the closing cupboard door. A moment later Rue heard ropes and pulleys set into motion and her mother's voice became more and more distant as she seemed to descend through the floor.

The Earl of Charleton jerked at Rue's arm and pulled her rudely down the stairs. Her ankles banged brutally against the hard steps as he forced her downward. Within moments they were in a darkened cellar.

Kablukov had taken the stairs as well, and now he huffed to a stop behind them.

"Over here," he said.

He stepped to the wall and opened a large cupboard door much like the one behind which Rue's mother had disappeared. He pulled the door wider and Rue's mother practically fell out into his arms.

"*Mamochka!*"

Rue tore herself away from Maclyn and lurched forward to keep her mother from falling to the floor. But Maclyn grabbed at her, tearing the red shawl from her shoulders. He kicked it away as it fell to the floor.

Rue screamed and pummeled at his chest, but he cruelly grabbed her wrists and dragged her along, following Kablukov who half-carried Rue's mother.

Without warning, Rue and her mother were shoved into a storage room. Water pipes clanked overhead as the two men tied the women's hands and feet.

"Where are the jewels?"

Maclyn towered over her, threatening her with his fists.

"I not know," she said through gritted teeth.

"Tell me!"

"I know nothing!"

She prayed she'd been convincing, even though the band of jewels sat like a beacon around her head.

He swung his arm and cuffed her hard. Her head slammed back against the pipes, loosening her hairpins and letting the heavy linen band slip dangerously.

Rue gasped and shrank as far as she could from his fists.

"We not know!" she insisted, though telling him would have been a blessing, if he'd just take the jewels and leave.

"We're wasting time. Give them the stuff," Maclyn ordered. "I'll go get Rathmore's daughter."

He kicked Rue's skirts aside as he made his way to the door and disappeared.

"Take off your clothes."

"Yevgeny! No! You must not do this." Rue's mother rose to her knees to clutch at Kablukov's hand. With one hand he fingered her bound wrists, and with other he reached to caress her cheek.

"Do as I say, Katka, and your daughter will live."

His cool words set Rue's heart trembling. Now he turned to Rue. "Both of you, do as I say. Remove your clothing down to your chemises." His fatherly face transformed as he spoke, leaving nothing but brutish intimidation in place of its former kindness.

"Yevgeny, you are a good man. You're not like that...that beast. Untie us and—"

"I can't."

"You must! Before he kills us. Kills *you*!"

Kablukov huffed. "He won't kill me."

"How can you know this," Katerina cried.

"Because he's my son!"

Silence consumed them as Rue and her mother considered the unlikely possibility that Kablukov and the Earl of Charleton could be father and son.

"Disrobe. Now."

Rue turned to her mother who sank back to the floor. Her eyes seemed to plead with her daughter to do what the man asked. But this couldn't possibly be happening. She'd come to the hospital to collect her mother and had merely stopped to check on Ned's friend. What kind of cruel fate had allowed her to cast her mother into this kind of danger?

Her mother lifted Rue's shaking hand and began to undo the buttons at her wrists. But she worked slowly. Ever so slowly. As if the longer she took, the sooner help might arrive.

"How I...how I do this?"

Rue's lips trembled as she held her wrists up to show him there was no way to remove her clothing if her hands were bound.

He muttered to himself as he drew a cruel-looking knife

from his pocket. With slashes as clean and accurate as a surgeon's, he slit her bodice in all the right places until it slid away. His moves seemed natural, as if he didn't have to think about it. As if he'd done it countless times before. Then he did the same for Katerina. The offhand cruelty of his movements sent a shiver through Rue which penetrated her bones.

As they sat trembling on the floor, Kablukov drew a blue vial from his coat pocket, pulled out the stopper, and held the vial to Rue's lips.

She drew back, stunned. "Vat iss?"

"Just drink it, pretty thing."

Disgust brought bile to her throat.

"You to drink first," Rue spat, knowing even as she spoke the words how futile they were.

"You'll drink it if you want your mother to see her homeland again."

Rue choked as she looked into the steely gaze of the man she thought had been a friend to them.

"Yevgeny Kablukov iss evil beast."

She swatted the bottle away as she issued her insult, startling the doctor and causing him to spill a good portion of liquid from the blue vial onto his hands. Droplets splashed on the toes of his highly polished shoes and dripped down the sides to stain the stone floor beneath his feet.

Kablukov uttered a sound that could only be recognized as fright. He set the sticky vial on a stack of crates and hastily retrieved his handkerchief. He spoke angrily as he furiously wiped the residue from his fingers.

"If you had just left with your mother, none of this would be happening. Why did you not leave?" Kablukov shifted and wiped his brow, shaking his head in a way that seemed almost sad.

Beside her, Katerina had unbuttoned her skirt and shoved it awkwardly to the floor. Rue recognized her bold movements for what they were. She was trying to take the man's attention off Rue and onto herself.

"So poor little doctor want jewels, yes?"

Kablukov swung on her. "What could a spoiled little rich girl possibly know of this?"

He threw his stained handkerchief angrily to the floor and continued to speak, though his voice was suddenly rough, sarcastic. Even accusing.

Rue started to speak, but he slashed a hand angrily through the air between them.

"Enough!"

A long silence settled over the three.

"Now drink. Or die. I really don't care which."

If she thought he could possibly mean to kill them, Rue would have given them the jewels that very moment. But it was unthinkable.

Kablukov reached out for the blue vial. Rue timed her kick perfectly and knocked her feet into the pile of crates. The vial teetered as Kablukov grappled for it. But the bottle eluded him, tipped, and spilled its contents over the tumbling crates.

Kablukov swore as he grabbed up the vial that was mostly drained.

"You will regret this," he growled.

With his face utterly transformed in anger, Kablukov seized Katerina's jaw, tipped her head back mercilessly, and poured what liquid remained in the blue vial down her throat. She sputtered, Rue screamed, and Kablukov stood back to gloat.

At that moment, Devan Maclyn charged through the door.

"She's gone!"

"Who—"

"Lady Georgiana. The night watchman says an orderly took a sick woman away in a carriage. Had to be her."

Kablukov grabbed Maclyn by the front of his waistcoat.

"Damn you worthless fop! Find her!"

He shoved Maclyn back through the door.

"What about these two?"

Kablukov growled. "Take this one to the sea salt salon." He indicated Rue's mother, who was now slumped against the wall, falling into a drugged sleep. Then he turned his eyes on Rue.

"I'll deal with this one."

Kablukov followed Maclyn into the hall and lowered his voice. But Rue heard every shocking word as if he'd stood just inches from her. And they chilled her to the bone.

Don't kill her until she tells you where the jewels are.

~~~

Ned called for his butler to warm some honey-laced brandy while he and Sol carefully settled Georgi on the settee in the front drawing room. She was incredibly weak and shaking uncontrollably from the ordeal. Sol drew a knitted throw around Georgi's shoulders while Ned threw fresh coal into the brazier. It seemed like his worst nightmare, finding Georgi collapsed on the floor, frightened out of her wits.

"Don't bother with me! You've got to help those women!"

Her voice was weak, thready, and drained of strength. The

effort of traveling here from the sanatorium had used every ounce of her reserves.

"What's happened!"

"Hold me, Sol. Please! Hold me! It's so awful!"

Sol knelt on the carpet, holding Georgi's hand in both of his.

Georgi's words came out in a rush, powered by sheer urgency.

"I had been waking for some time, you know, opening my eyes and then falling back to sleep. I didn't know what day it was, or even where I was. But I felt I was safe. Then out of nowhere something crashed to the floor nearby, and there was shouting on the other side of the wall, and it...it seemed to drag me fully awake." She looked at both men. "The voices were so angry. And Sol! They were talking about our expedition!"

"Georgi, that...that's unlikely." Both men looked at one another, each of them doubting that Georgi could have actually heard what she was reporting to have heard.

"But it's true! Miss Charkova and her mother will tell you!"

"Wait, Georgi. What were they doing there?"

"I...I don't...you have to believe me! They were there."

"Alright, alright, we believe you. And they heard what you heard?"

"Yes! They were as stunned as I was. The one man was mad at the other for not getting rid of my body. Sol, he said they threw all the bodies overboard except for...except for me." She clutched at Sol's leather vest. "They knew everything!"

She sobbed.

Sol stroked her cheek. "Let me understand this. You heard someone talking, and it frightened you, so you left? To come here?"

"No, Sol! A nurse called for the doctor and...and when he

came, the Earl of Charleton was with him."

"What? That makes no sense!"

Ned and Sol exchanged a worried glance. Her raving now sounded simply delusional.

"It was him! Don't you see? Somehow he and that doctor knew about the jewels. It was their men who attacked us! And then...and then Devan recognized me. It's my fault they have Rue and her mother!"

Now she seemed truly deranged.

"Georgi, calm yourself. Don't you see? You must have dreamed it all."

"It wasn't a dream!"

Sol stroked her cheek. "Now, now. Take it easy. Just help us understand, darling."

Georgi clutched at Sol's hands as she drew a long, trembling breath.

"I heard the voices talking about the expedition, and I must have fainted. But then Miss Charkova brought her mother in a wheelchair to see me and it bumped into the bed and woke me again. I was awake, Sol. I was awake! And I...I knew I had to tell them what I heard, so they could warn you not to come back to the sanatorium."

Alarm landed like a boulder on Ned's chest each time he heard Rue's name.

Georgi laid her hand over Sol's. "If you came tonight while those men were there, they might recognize you. So I told Miss Charkova as much as I could. And I..." she stopped, like a child afraid to admit what she'd done. "I gave her the *Stones of Saqqarah*."

Ned's heart plummeted. An entire ship's crew had been

murdered for the very jewels that were now in Rue's possession. He feared for her like he'd never feared for anything in his life. He wanted to fly like the wind to her side, to shield her, to carry her to safety. To chuck the damned jewels in the Thames.

He turned and saw Sol's face transform. "You had the jewels? On you? All this time?"

"In my hair," she said, her voice breaking, "wrapped in that laced linen hair decoration. It started to slip off and I realized what I needed to do. I made Miss Charkova put it in her own hair, thinking she'd leave withit. But then, oh dear lord, it was awful. A nurse pulled back the curtain and saw that I had wakened. She called for the doctor and in just a few seconds he was there. He had come from the room on the other side of the wall! I recognized his voice right away. He saw how frightened we were and he knew. He knew we had heard." She clutched at Sol's hand, but looked at Ned. "We were all staring at him, Ned. Frightened to death. And then...then the other man stepped in through the curtains and I knew things were going to get worse."

"Why? Because you knew him?"

She nodded. "I told you, Neddie. It was Maclyn!"

"Maclyn." Ned scoffed. "What the hell would he have to do with this?"

"He's gone crazy, Ned. I swear! He and the doctor dragged Rue and her mother away, and they were coming back for me! I did the only thing I could do. I fainted back against the pillow until they were gone. You have to get there! Now! Before they do something dreadful!"

If there were even the smallest shred of truth in her story, he had to do something. Ned ran a frustrated hand through his hair. Nobody knew where Rue was. Could it be that Georgi was right?

Ned sprang to his feet. "We're going, Georgi. But do you have any idea where they went? Out of the building? Into the doctor's study?"

"I don't know, Neddie. All I heard was the women screaming and trying to get away."

Ned threw on his coat and bolted for the door. Her words tore at his heart. How terrified they must have been. Might still be. "Is there anything else, Georgi? Anything at all?"

"Oh yes! Neddie, I did hear something else!"

He stopped short. "What?"

"It sounded like ropes, or buckets, you know, like something going down into a well."

CHAPTER NINE

EVERY SOUND OF THEIR STRUGGLE was magnified ten-fold as it bounced off the cellar pipes that traced the underbelly of *Rosehaven Sanatorium.*

Kablukov dragged Rue by the twisted rope that bound her hands, pulling her roughly along the passageway.

"No do this! Please!"

Kablukov stopped pulling and turned to her. "Tell me where the girl has gone and I'll let you go."

Rue saw the lie in his eyes.

"How I know this? I cannot say what I not know!"

She felt the trickle of tears wet her cheeks and willed them to stop. Her answer angered the man, and he jerked her roughly through a door. She stumbled across the door sill, but when she righted herself she was stunned. They had moved out of the dark cellar passageway and into a beautiful room. Lovely painted tiles led the way to several copper baths, each fringed with elegant sheer ivory curtains. Fine artwork in gilded frames graced every wall, and each wall was tastefully covered in gold damask. Over each bath hung a chandelier, not lit, but reflecting light that flickered elsewhere in the room. The lighting perfectly graced the sitting areas where elegant settees were grouped for conversation. But the light dimmed over the baths, lending privacy beyond the sheer curtains.

The startling difference between this lavish room and the rest of the rather stark sanatorium showed quite clearly that this was a private place. For London's most prestigious clientele.

Rue's beautiful mother lay in the third bath, looking for all the world like she belonged there. She lay half submerged, her lovely hair splaying out over the copper back of the tub. Maclyn knelt beside the bath, securing a pretty leather vest about her upper body. Her chemise and knickers bubbled about in the water that seemed to churn a bit, sending steam into the room lit with a hundred small frosted lanterns.

As they passed the two empty baths, Rue felt a stone of fear rise into her throat. Each bath had an identical leather vest, each painted with flowers that twined about, making something pretty out of a thing meant to imprison. Each vest was secured with gleaming brass bolts to the back of its copper tub.

She shivered. One would have to know how the thing worked if she hoped to get free of it.

With a mean jerk, Kablukov stopped her in front of her mother.

"She is beautiful, is she not?"

His voice held a surprising bit of awe. Rue stilled her own tongue. She wanted to scream at him to avert his eyes, that he had no right to appreciate a woman as pure as her mother. But she would not give him the satisfaction of showing her emotions, when that is exactly what his action was purposefully designed to do.

He nodded some kind of signal to Maclyn, and the young earl immediately rose and walked to Rue's side. He sneered as he took harsh hold of the rope that bound her hands.

Kablukov walked to the head of the bath.

"Like Sleeping Beauty, don't you think?"

He reached out a hand to lift a long tress of Katerina's hair, kneeling as he did so, and raised the lovely curls to his lips. He breathed deeply, making Rue want to scream in fury. But she held her tongue.

Not far from Katerina's head, a dozen colorful atomizers and perfume bottles were prettily arranged on a small silver tray.

"She mustn't stay in here too long, you know."

He reached for a red crystal bottle, then seemed to take delicious joy in pulling the stopper and allowing a few powdery grains to fall into the water.

"Just a bit will keep her complexion perfectly snowy," he smiled. "But too much? Tsk tsk. Too much could be, shall we say...fatal?"

Could it be arsenic? Everyone knew of its potent—and potentially deadly—effect. Even her mother worked a few grains of it into her face creams. It kept her skin looking soft and fresh as a newborn babe. Judging from the delight Kablukov took in spilling it into the bath, Rue feared he was adding far too much. Her lips barely parted as she whispered, "Stop. Stop now."

"Ah, I would, my dear, and I could...if you would just tell me what I need to know. So where? Where do you think the dear Lady Georgiana might have taken the jewels?"

Rue swallowed.

Things were now at a tipping point. She had to tell him something.

"She...she go to town house in Mayfair. Or...to Solomon Rockefeller."

Maclyn shook her roughly. "She wouldn't go to the Mayfair house. She knows we'd find her there. And Rockefeller's dead, so a lot of good that will do her. Try again."

Rue faced him and watched madness curl Maclyn's lip into an ugly sneer.

"Zis iss where you are wrong."

She smiled, knowing she could impart information that would shock both men and perhaps throw them off their guard.

"Solomon Rockefeller lives."

~~~

It neared midnight as Ned and Sol raced their horses through London streets, desperate to reach Rosehaven before something terrible happed to Rue. And her mother.

Lines of carriages collecting their passengers at opera houses and theatres made frustrating obstacles that slowed them, until they reached the trade canal that they knew stretched way beyond their destination. Now they urged their horses to a full run, speeding along the track that bordered the canal. The occasional pedestrian made all haste to get out of their way.

Rosehaven was essentially dark when they reached it, with just a few windows lit by low-burning nightlights.

Both men leaped from their horses and sped up the steps and into the reception hall.

"Where was her bed?"

Sol called out the location as they ran stride for stride down the hall. "This way!" An exhausted attendant made a half-hearted attempt to stop them, but they barreled on.

It was just as Georgi had said. A series of private rooms, then a room with the doctor's name etched on the doorplate. And then the row of curtained hospital beds. There was little to draw attention that something sinister had happened here, except for a metal pan upside down on the floor and an overturned bedside table.

At that moment the sound of creaking pulleys filtered into the hall. Ned backed out of the curtain and looked in every direction. It was just as Georgi had said. Like the sound of ropes and buckets. But where—?

Ned called to Sol as he sped toward the sound.

It took only seconds to determine the sound was coming from behind the paneling at the end of the corridor. Ned grabbed at the only door latch and pulled, only to see two sets of ropes—one moving upward, and one moving down.

"It's…it's like a pantry lift! Quick! Downstairs! They must be in the cellar!"

The two charged down the stairs, turned at the landing, and descended further. Together they reached the stone floor and lurched around the corner, only to stop abruptly.

A young girl was just opening a cupboard door to reach for a large basket of soiled linens. As she lifted the basket out, Ned grabbed her harshly by the arm.

The girl turned in shock and uttered a fearful cry.

Ned tried to bury his own fear at what he saw.

"Easy, my man," Sol warned. "She's just a kid."

"A kid. Yes," Ned growled. "And she's wearing Rue's shawl."

~~~

Rue smiled at the shock on Maclyn's face.

"You're lying. Rockefeller can't be alive," Maclyn growled.

"He pull himself from water and save Lady Georgiana. How you think half-dead girl get here? On carpet of magic?"

Her quip made him angry, and Maclyn slapped her hard.

It only fueled her anger.

"He here. He come with me to bring Lady Georgiana." She laughed. "Right under you nose. And you not even know he here!"

Maclyn slapped her again. She lifted her bound hands to her burning cheek.

"My Ned iss wrong. You not unscrupulous cad. You son of Devil."

It was the wrong thing to say. Maclyn let loose an angry torrent and threw her violently to the floor. With her hands bound in front of her she couldn't protect herself. She landed hard, her head hitting half on the plush Aubusson carpet and half on the stone floor, jarring her pitifully.

And sending the linen band of jewels flying.

It, too, hit the floor.

The impact split the fine linen that had protected the jewels for more than six days. But now they poured out onto the floor.

One by one the *Stones of Saqqarah* came to rest at Kablukov's feet.

Maclyn growled out a whisper. "She had them all the time."

Kablukov bent to retrieve the stones.

Rue lay still, trying desperately to recover herself as Kablukov picked up each jewel, one by one, and dropped them into his coat pocket.

"I thought I might let you go, little one," he smiled. "For your mother's sake, you see. But you have taken things just a bit too far and I'm afraid it's over now."

Kablukov stood and put his foot down hard upon the rope that bound her hands.

Maclyn backed away.

Kablukov looked at Rue for a long moment, and without looking away, issued his command to Maclyn.

"Turn on the water."

Devan Maclyn smiled, for some reason delighted to comply. He moved with theatrical grace to the head of the copper bath where her mother lay and turned the spigot. Around and around he turned it, until the metal lever came away in his hand. Water flowed harder and harder as it fairly gushed into the tub.

Rue gasped. It only took her a moment to assess what was about to happen. Her mother lay with her head against the foot of the tub, unconscious, and secured to the tub with the restraining vest. The water was already rising. It would only take minutes for it to reach her mother's chin. And long before it spilled over the top of the tub, her mother would drown.

"Noooooooooo!"

CHAPTER TEN

THE GIRL WEARING RUE'S SHAWL was no help at all. She'd simply found the pretty thing abandoned on the floor near the lift cupboard. The ends of the pretty red shawl hung unevenly from the scrawny laundress's shoulder. When Ned looked closer, he saw the reason.

Rue's shawl was torn.

Just as he was about to draw the shawl away from the girl, a faraway scream jolted him into action.

He tore down the hallway with Sol's booted feet pounding close behind. He skidded to a stop when they came upon an open door. Broken blue glass littered the floor and a few crates had tumbled this way and that. Two sets of lovely clothing lay scattered about, each of them cut to shreds. He recognized one as the walking suit Rue had been wearing for their drive in the park that very morning. Ned froze momentarily at the sight of it, but some corner of his brain registered that it was not as bad as it might be. At least there was no blood.

But Rue and her mother had been here alright. And recently. The spilled liquid was still wet.

Stop! Please! I begging you!

It was Rue! And she was closer now.

They followed the sound through the cellar tunnel, each turn taking them deeper into darkness. Ned crashed into hard boiler pipes and rough wooden braces, each one leaving its mark. But he felt nothing. Except fear.

When they saw light spilling beneath a door, Ned halted and put out his hand to Sol. They crept to the door and knew instantly they had found the women.

Rue was crying hysterically.

Stop water! Please! Stop it!

Ned drew his pistol and whispered. "Open the door."

Sol complied, opening the door wide enough that Ned could look in and assess what was happening. But when he saw Maclyn wrestling with Rue, he bolted inside.

"Let her go, you bastard!"

Maclyn froze, then turned to him with a diabolical smile.

"So you can what, Danton? Waltz away with her?" He pulled Rue tightly to him and raised a knife point to the base of her neck.

"My Ned, they—"

Danton silenced her by touching the knife to her skin.

"You hurt her and I'll see you hang, Maclyn."

The doctor he had met just that morning stepped out of a curtained area.

"You'll have to find us first, my good man." He grabbed Rue by the rope that bound her and pulled her roughly to him, leaving Maclyn free to attack.

"Take him down, son."

Maclyn leaped forward and Ned got off a shot. But Maclyn

charged headlong into him, still wielding his knife. Ned twisted and kicked, using every method he'd learned about defending himself from a hoodlum.

But Maclyn was no hoodlum. He was fast. Nimble.

Ned knew he was no match for this devil.

~~~

Rue struggled as Kablukov dragged her away from the fight. He had his hand clamped roughly across her mouth, making it hard for her to breathe. And impossible to scream.

But suddenly his hand fell away and she was pushed roughly to the ground.

She turned her head in time to see Sol Rockefeller grappling with the doctor. How ever it was that he had managed to get into the room without calling attention to himself was a mystery. But she thanked every god she knew that he had. She slid as far away as she could, then scrambled to her feet. She had to get to her mother!

But the men took a long twisting roll and passed right in front of her.

Sol grabbed Kablukov by the jacket and began pounding on his face until the man got hold of the end of the tub next to her mother's. For the first time, Rue realized there was water in that tub, too. They'd intended to drown her as well, hadn't they.

Her heart was racing at breakneck speed now as she dashed past the skirmish. But not before she saw Sol rip away the pocket of Kablukov's coat. In a glittering arc of glimmering color, the *Stones of Saqqarah* tumbled into the water.

Kablukov screamed.

That was the last she heard as she raced through the curtains and into the adjacent bathing chamber, then clamped a hand over her mouth to stifle her own scream. The water was almost to her mother's chin.

Rue plunged her bound hands into the water and wrestled with the buckled straps of the vest that bound her mother to the tub. Her numb fingers searched frantically, but with the churning water and the fabric from her mother's chemise bubbling about, she couldn't feel a way to undo the horrid thing.

She felt her heart might burst at the thought that any second she might lose her mother to the threatening water.

Leave the vest. Stop the water!

The voice in her head seemed outrageously calm. She'd wasted precious seconds, but now knew that if she couldn't get her mother loose, all she had to do was stop the flowing water. She lunged to the other end of the tub where the water was pouring in, and sobbed. The spigot handle had been ripped away. There was no way to turn off the flow of the killing waterfall. She plunged her hands into the water and clawed at the drain plug, but the mechanism seemed frozen in place and refused to budge.

Rue turned in a frantic circle. There must be a way. And then she saw the answer. The silver tray. She grabbed it up, sending the lovely perfume atomizers and crystal vials crashing to the floor. She thrust the tray under the spouting water and angled it toward the nearest edge of the tub.

It didn't reach.

She began using it like a scoop to bail water over the side, until she realized she was making small waves that were splashing as high as her mother's nose.

"Stop."

Her mother's quiet voice could barely be heard above the din in the room. The splashing water had roused her mother who realized in an instant her state of peril.

"Please stop."

Katerina lifted her chin, somehow knowing even in her semi-conscious state that it was the only way she would survive the rising waters. Her hands flailed at the tub as she sought to pull herself out of danger.

"*Mamochka!*" Rusilla felt her scream lodge in her own throat. She scooped water more gently, but it wasn't enough! She had to get more water out of the tub.

And then a small scene from her childhood flashed into her mind. Once, when she had felt particularly playful, she had entered her nightly bath by running across the room and jumping in. She had displaced more water than she had left in the small tub.

Would it work? Would it be enough? Would it backfire on her and simply hasten her mother's death?

Without pausing, she sat with her back to the tub and with all her might, threw herself sideways into the water. Bucketfuls of water sloshed over the side. She struggled to get hold of the copper tub's edge and only managed to get to her knees. It had helped! Now she used her bound hands to bail water, sending wave after wave of water out of the copper bath.

"Rue."

She felt a hand on her shoulder, but she wasn't done yet. There was still water pouring into the tub from the damaged spigot.

"Rue?"

"It working!" She sobbed. "It working!"

"Rue. Sweetheart. You can stop now."

She couldn't believe him. But a moment later she heard a change in the sound of the rushing water. It was no longer coming into the tub. She stopped bailing and turned to see that Sol had secured a large piece of wood paneling to act as a sluice and divert the water onto the floor.

"Clever setup, I should say. I wouldn't mind having one of these contraptions—" Solomon Rockefeller caught her look of horror and didn't finish his sentence. "I'll go find the source and turn off the water," he said as he wiped his bloody brow.

Rue turned the other direction to see Ned half in the tub beside her. He had the vest undone and was beginning to lift her mother from the tub.

"You saved her, Rue."

"She iss alright?"

"Yes, sweetheart, though she seems to have fainted."

"He make her sleep," Rue cried. "With blue bottle."

Ned nodded as if he understood. He lifted Katerina's wet body from the tub and laid her on the nearest settee. With one swift pull he dragged down a large length of curtain to cover her with.

Then he turned to Rue.

She still knelt in the tub, too weak to rise, until Ned put his strong arms around her waist and lifted her into his arms. Her soaked chemise and knickers gave worthless cover as she pressed herself to him.

He turned away from the tub and drew her higher until she could raise her bound hands over his head and clasp him around the neck. She buried her face in the warmth of his shoulder and sobbed.

"Sh," he whispered. "Hush now. You've saved your mother. And you're free."

"I free." She lifted her head. "I free."

She lifted her hands back from around his neck and for the first time looked about. The men who had killed Georgi's father and tried to kill her and her mother were nowhere in sight.

"How?"

"Maclyn is tied up. He'll probably spend the rest of his days in prison."

Rue took a long breath. "Kablukov?"

When she leaned back a bit to look into his eyes, he carried her to a settee opposite her mother and sat down with Rue still on his lap. He tenderly brushed the sodden curls away from her face. As gently as if she were a small child, Ned began to loosen the painful ropes that bound her hands. He was silent for a moment as he removed the rope and cast it away.

"Kablukov went after the *Stones of Saqqarah*."

"They fall in water."

"Yes, in the bath. Sol struggled with him and he...drowned."

Rue sighed, a long, agonizing release of anxiety. How sad that greed had ruined what could have been a good man. And how sad that Solomon Rockefeller would have to carry such a tragic memory in his soul.

She looked Ned in the eye to make sure he heard what she said next. "You must to throw away *Stones of Saqqarah*."

"Rue—"

"*Nyet*! I mean this! They are curse! They only to kill!" She began to feel a bit of panic rising to her throat. "Do not touch them, my Ned. Please!"

"Hush now. They're in the tub. We'll collect them and leave them for the authorities."

He gently set her on her feet and together they moved arm in arm to the tub that had been intended to end Rue's life and instead had taken the life of the doctor. They stopped abruptly, expecting to see a tub of water with six great emeralds and a bevy of diamonds glittering on the tub's floor. Instead, they gazed in shock at the empty tub that sat gleaming in the chandelier light—devoid of water, devoid of jewels. Nothing but a shiny expanse of copper.

Ned spoke in little more than a whisper. "I didn't touch them, Rue. I swear."

She looked around swiftly. Did that mean Solomon had them?

But he stopped her with a hand on her cheek.

"When Sol struggled with Kablukov, the man managed to open the drain thinking he could save himself from drowning. But it was too late. Sol held him to the end. And when he pulled Kablukov out of the tub, the drain must have stayed open, and the water took the *Stones of Saqqarah* down the drain."

Rue let go of Ned's hand. Just letting him go started her trembling all over again.

"Now they are where they belong," she whispered.

She felt Ned's arms come around her, and she turned into him.

"And now it's time for you to go where *you* belong," he whispered back.

"Oh yes," she sighed. "Now we take my *mamochka* home."

He smiled. "Yes, we'll take your *mamochka* home."

She searched his eyes to see if he felt what she did, and when it took only a fleeting second to confirm it, she lifted her face to him, and he lowered his to her.

And they kissed, a long, warm, desperately comforting kiss she hoped would never end.

Chapter Eleven

SEVEN DAYS PASSED BEFORE RUE could be convinced to consider leaving the house. The entire Wayburton family had rallied around her and her mother like their own personal army. Even the staff guarded them, never leaving them alone for so much as a minute, until at last Rue began to feel safe.

Sol appeared occasionally to share a meal and report on Lady Georgiana's recovery. At last she seemed to be gaining strength, and he wouldn't stay away from her any longer than absolutely necessary.

Just the day before, he had sat with them and revealed the outcome of a major excavating project he'd helped with. In the cellar of *Rosehaven Sanatorium.*

"First they pulled out the copper tub and examined the drain, and they did find one smallish eight-carat diamond."

"Then the *Stones of Saqqarah* did go down the drain," Ned said with a satisfied smile.

"Well, I don't think so. They reamed out a pipe that leads to a large canal that empties into the Thames. There wasn't a single jewel anywhere in the length of the pipe, or in the sluice where it falls into the canal. Not a one."

"That...that's surprising."

Ned was studying Solomon, who was gazing back at him with a look that could only be described as wary.

"One might think you..." Ned started to voice the unthinkable, and the implication made Solomon bolt to his feet.

"No, man. I did *not* take the jewels. And I expect you to swear on your honor that you didn't either."

Now Ned rose swiftly, offended by his friend's accusation. "Of course I did not. They had to have gone down the drain, Sol. They *had* to."

Rue looked at Solomon Rockefeller. Could he by lying? Had he taken the jewels while Ned was rescuing her? It didn't seem possible. And looking at the disappointment on his face, she couldn't believe he could be lying about it.

Ned extended his hand stiffly, offering his handshake to seal the oath between friends. Long seconds passed, and then, without a word, and without extending his own hand, Sol turned and strode from the room.

It had been an ugly moment. Each of them had felt the other to be a man of integrity. And yet, in the aftermath of an unexplainable event, both held the other in suspicion.

It had been an awkward, uncomfortably tense moment. And for the life of her, Rue could not see a way to exonerate either of the men.

Now, a full day later, Rue sat on a loveseat in the morning room, as close to Ned as propriety would allow. Perhaps closer. Everyone seemed to respect the bond between them that was sealed when Ned saved her from certain death. They honored the sanctity of it by allowing the couple extraordinary space.

Extraordinary privacy. But always with their defenders hovering just beyond the doors.

Even her mother seemed to indicate that the only time she could take her eyes off her daughter was when a certain handsome young duke was at Rue's side.

But he would be leaving soon. The diplomatic trip to the Suez would take him away from her.

Today Rue had brought her balalaika to the drawing room, intending to lift both their spirits and dispel the undercurrent of worry. It began well, but by the second tune she realized she was choosing somber melodies, and that had not been her intention. All day she'd felt the need to break from the restrictive rhythms of survival and just breathe.

Rue took a long, measured breath and realized if she didn't move now, she'd be bound in this state of victimhood forever, as surely as Kablukov had bound her hands with rope. She quietly laid the balalaika aside and reached a hand to comfort the wrist that still troubled her most. Its burns were less reddened and raw today, but still bothersome.

"Is big quiet," she sighed. Rue stood up and stepped away from Ned. "Too much quiet."

Ned chuckled. "You prefer mayhem, sweetheart?"

She turned, puzzled by the new word he'd used.

He ran a hand through his hair as if he were thinking how best to define *mayhem* for her.

"It's when everything goes all collywobbles and widdershins," he said with a sly wink.

Her eyebrows screwed even higher. "My Neddie, you confuse this girl."

She pouted, prompting him to laugh—a full, long, easy

laugh. As it filled the room, she realized it had been a week since he'd managed to do such a thing. To laugh.

Ned stepped close to her and placed a hand on each of her arms, just below her shoulders, and began to move his thumbs in a soft caress.

"When something goes all *collywobbles*, it's making a person feel afraid. Worried."

He didn't look at her, but seemed to concentrate on his thumbs, as if they wanted to wander further afield.

"And *widdershins* is like...backwards. Counterclockwise." He stopped the motion of his thumbs and reversed the direction of his caress.

Rue gasped. If she didn't step away from his sensuous touch she was going to shatter into a million pieces.

She bit her lower lip.

"*Collyshins* and *wibble wobbles*. Iss funny words."

She was startled at how much breath it took to speak those few words. Rue commanded herself to find the strength to step away from his hands that so aroused her, but not a single muscle moved.

She pressed her lips together, hoping to stop her lower lip from trembling. But the movement drew Ned's eyes, sending the tremble all the way to the tips of her fingers. His rotating thumbs paused, then slid up her arms, across her shoulders, and upward until he cradled her face in the palms of his hands.

Her own hands flew to his chest, but not to push him away. Instead, they simply clutched at his brocade waistcoat as he lifted her face.

All thinking ceased as his lips captured hers.

Her heart thundered as his hands drew her face even closer,

demanding that she rise to the tips of her toes to meet him with all the eagerness her body willed. The kiss seemed to know its own need as Rue simply gave herself to it. To him. To the rapture he was seeding within her.

She sensed his regret as Ned at last drew away. But something strange was happening to her. Even as his lips separated from hers, a connection remained. She felt it in the furthest reaches of her soul.

And it made her smile.

For the first time in many days, joy returned. Ned's glorious kiss had washed away the trauma. She felt alive in a way she'd never felt before.

But it was hardly fair of her to require Ned's constant presence to make her feel whole. She would not be his burden. She must no longer rely on something or someone else to restore her spirits. She had to do this for herself. And for Ned.

"Iss no good, my Ned."

He attempted to draw her closer but she swept out a hand to keep him at a distance.

"Rue? What do you mean, it's no good?"

His voice took on a sudden worried tone and she turned to him with a smile meant to reassure him that he had no need to worry. She wasn't stepping away from him, she was stepping away from this gloomy mood.

"Iss no good to live like this...live in worry, live every day with fear. It eat my very heart!"

Ned nodded and waited for her to continue. He had such a gift for that, for knowing when to speak and when to listen. It was one of his dearest traits.

"So I leaving."

Now his face fell back into its wary expression.

"Leaving? You're leaving?"

"Yes! I leaving! I leaving this room. I leaving this house. I leaving this prison."

"But why?"

She huffed.

"Because, my Ned, I am Rusilla Ivanovna Charkova. I not coward. I not little shrinking violet. I strong. Like sword."

She stepped toward him.

"*You* see me, my Ned. I know it. You see who is me. I not break."

She let out a long breath, like a great, sighing purge.

"I not break."

Ned stepped closer and took her hands in his. With this simple act, Rue felt the last small residue of fear fall away.

"You're right, my love." He lowered his face to hers and kissed her forehead. "You *are* strong." He kissed her cheek. "Like a sword tempered in the flame." He kissed the bridge of her nose and brought laughter to her lips. "Well. Maybe not a sword." He clucked his tongue at her. "Maybe more like a little silver butter knife."

He ran his hands up her arms, sending wave upon wave of rejuvenating want through her limbs. "But a very powerful, very Russian little butter knife." He winked.

Now he had both of them laughing until Rue planted her hands on his chest.

"But little Russian butter knife need to be in world. Need to make life! Iss why I must go."

Ned blinked several times and cocked his head, not understanding.

"Rue. Darling. Don't torture me. Go where?"

Rue felt her smile sail up from her very toes to light her face as she held out a small, square, elegantly inscribed card.

"To the ball, my silly Ned. Of course that iss where we go! To Devington Ball!"

~~~

Little more than four hours later, Rue walked into the Devingtons' grand Mayfair ballroom on Ned's arm. He seemed as delighted as she was to be back in a normal situation, back in a place where there were rules, and one had only to know the rules to feel completely at home.

It seemed a thousand candles had been conscripted to light the night. Every surface in the grand mansion sparkled, reflecting the elegant curves of intricate sconces and catching the glint of silver polished to a high sheen.

Every bit of it proclaimed the delight to be found in swishing gowns twirling to dazzling music.

Yet for Rue, the joy of tonight was having Ned by her side, Ned brushing her shoulder, Ned whose eyes glinted as they lingered overlong on her face.

The quadrille suddenly became a sensuous dance, with breathtaking moments of turning and touching. And the waltz, oh, the waltz completely changed from whirling and swaying to merely floating on air.

Rue found herself unable to pull her eyes away from Ned to take in the room. All around her, gowns swayed and shiny boots and dress patens whispered across the floor. She felt them. She heard them. But she only had eyes for one man, and he for her.

It seemed that nobody dared separate them. Or perhaps they tried and neither Ned nor Rue noticed. In fact, they'd broken the 'rule of four' which Society had long enforced. They'd danced together five times already, and had only forced themselves to dance with others once, for the sake of appearances.

Through much of the first half of the evening, the only moments they weren't touching one another were those moments when the dance steps required that they move apart.

But even that was something Rue began to look forward to, because it made the coming back together all the more thrilling. All evening she found herself sending him coy, flirtatious looks she didn't even know she knew.

"We're going to have to be grown-ups for a bit, my love," Ned whispered in her ear.

Rue scoffed. "My silly Ned, why you say such unhappy thing?"

He laughed. "It's time for cigars and a bit of cards."

Rue began to object.

"Ah, ah, ah," he chided. "I adore you but I am not brave enough to be the only fellow among this gaggle of geese." He swept his hand about the room and she saw groups of women already moving toward the parlors where they would find refreshment. "Lovely as they are."

In truth, Rue saw that it was a bit of a crush, and it would only be unkind of her to make him suffer through it. She would retire with the women and let Ned find the cardroom. In an hour he would be returning to find her. She had no doubt of it.

"Rue! Come along with us!" A chorus of feminine voices chimed a greeting in her ear. "We want to hear all about your daring escapade."

They took her by each arm and swept her along with them.

"Oh yes," cried another. "Were you frightened to death?"

Rue let the young women propel her as she turned her head to keep her eyes fixed on Ned. He still stood in the middle of the ballroom floor, one hand reaching slightly forward as if he might draw her back to him. The other lay handsomely over his heart, like a young cavalier about to step from a painting.

She knew him so thoroughly now, knew just how high she might have to reach her hand to touch his shoulder, how steadily she must walk to match his stride. How perfectly she fit beneath his arm.

And it had all happened so fast, in a matter of a few breathless days.

With a young countess on one side of her gowned in ivory sashed in pale blue, and a debutante on the other side in silver with cherry-pink bows, Rue felt like a hothouse flower in her simmering tangerine gown. But Ned had been captivated by it.

The girls whisked her past the doddering matrons and managed to be first at the mirrors in the women's retiring room where a conscientious maiden could powder her nose. Attendants hovered about, always ready with a bit of pristine linen just when it was needed.

The young women kept up their chatter as they clustered tightly about a gilded half-table.

"It's absolutely scandalous, Miss Charkova! Dancing every dance with the Duke of Wellbury? However did you find the nerve?"

The second girl leaned close to Rue's ear. "Are you loving it?"

Rue merely blushed.

"Of course she's loving it. How could she not? He's so...so..."

The first young lady paused to search for a word.

"Gallant," one supplied, nudging Rue.

"Yes, gallant, and..."

"Princely," another said, lowering her voice to an intimate tone.

"Oh yes! Gallant and princely and...and..."

"And altogether scrumptious," an exuberant young lady declared.

Rue reached a hand to pinch her cheeks and realized they were already aflame.

"Ladies," she said, surprised to hear a new maturity in her tone. "Iss kind of you to admire my Neddie, but no more. Now come. We refresh."

The girls exchanged a glance in the mirror. A natural instinct to respond as girls do was easy for Rue to squelch. Giggling and tittle-tattle no longer rose eagerly to her lips. Rather, she found herself enjoying a calm that swept through her body. It made her feel taller, lovelier, more graceful, and altogether more mature. She was far beyond swooning now. This felt like standing on the precipice of true love.

Rue hooked a hand through the elbows of the two chatty girls and moved with them across the hall to a table laden with French pastries, all done up in lacy white frosting. She selected one and moved along to a lush-looking bowl of fruit to capture a cascading stem of grapes. Just as she popped the first juicy orb into her mouth, Rue became aware of a careless conversation taking place nearby.

It's only an infatuation, child. The girl is merely exotic.

The dowager Countess of Mecklenhold stood just beyond the refreshment table, chatting with her granddaughter in a careless tone.

But Grandmama, she's so beautiful.

A rather ugly sound escaped the dowager's lips.

Beautiful you say? Well, I suppose she is. In a garish sort of way.

Rue angled her shoulders so that her eyes were not directed at the two women. She'd seen quite enough of the granddaughter recently. The girl seemed to be a permanent fixture at every card party, musicale, and dinner.

Thinking of the thin, big-eyed girl foisted a surprising recollection. She was actually the girl Ned had been so intent upon avoiding that first night at the ball masque. The night when he'd been so impatient to dance with Lady Georgiana that he had enlisted Rue's help.

What a fateful night that had been!

Rue smiled.

Have you spoken with the duke's aunt?

The girl's voice had taken on a wheedling tone.

Of course, dear, and you have nothing to worry your pretty head over. Lady Treadway assured me she will do all in her power to see that you become the Duchess of Wellbury.

A cough came on so harshly that Rue found herself struggling to breathe. *Duchess of Wellbury? That mewling child?* Rue hardly knew whether to laugh or cry. If the girl would just smile once in a while she might actually be halfway pretty. But could she catch the interest of a man like Ned? That was like asking if pigs could fly.

"Water, dear?"

Rue turned to see the dowager Countess of Mecklenhold at her shoulder, holding out a water goblet in her spindly, aged fingers.

"I...*Da*. Thank you." Rue took the goblet and drank eagerly, heedless of the droplets that splattered across her heated breast. Had she been caught eavesdropping?

"Gracious me, one would think you'd just returned from the Sahara," the dowager said.

Rue lowered the glass and swallowed. Her cough had quite disappeared.

"Iss better now."

The dowager gave her a furtive look, then drew her granddaughter to her side. "I trust you've met my granddaughter? Lady Eugenia Strothfield?"

Rue turned a warm smile on the woman's granddaughter who stood before her.

"Yes. I meet this little twit," she said.

She wasn't at all prepared for the reaction of the two women. Shock, horror, indignation. They all cascaded across the disapproving expressions launched on thin faces drawn back in disgust.

Why would they react like this? She'd used the term of endearment she'd so often heard. How could they have been offended?

"Shocking. Positively shocking," the dowager sputtered. "Come Eugenia!"

Without another word, the two women swept away, leaving Rue at the refreshment table wondering what in the world she'd done now.

~~~

Ned looked across the library table at his American friend. He'd had enough of cards, and when Solomon Rockefeller entered the room, he drew the fellow to the fireplace for a brandy. Sol was on edge, clearly no more comfortable in Ned's presence than Ned was in his.

"What are your plans now, if I may ask?" Ned raised his snifter in salute, then took a drink.

Sol returned the salute, which was a step in the right direction after having shunned Ned's handshake the day before.

"I was called to Chesterfield Gardens yesterday."

"Wait, the Egyptian consulate?"

Sol nodded.

"Cultural attaché. I'm to finish questioning the participants and turn everything over to them. They'll pursue finding the jewels."

Sol rubbed a hand across his forehead.

"I wouldn't want to be on the poking end of their stick, I can tell you that."

He gave a half-hearted laugh.

"Anyway, as soon as Georgiana is well enough, we'll leave for the States. I don't mind telling you I've had enough of this place."

As he spoke, Sol's eyes flitted sideways as if he wanted to catch Ned's reaction to his words but was unwilling to look him square in the eye.

"I thought you'd finished questioning Maclyn about Kablukov. There wasn't anyone else there, as near as I can recall."

Now Sol sat back and rested his brandy snifter on one knee. He studied it a moment before answering.

"Right. Maclyn, Kablukov, you, me, Katerina, and..."

For some reason he hesitated, and Ned saw his jaw tense, as if he were biting back the words he wanted to say.

"And Miss Charkova," Ned supplied.

Sol took a slow drink before answering.

"Yes. The lovely Miss Charkova."

Ned set his glass on the table and leaned forward. "Don't be daft, Rockefeller. Rue has told us everything she knows."

Sol pierced him with an accusatory look. "Has she?"

"You know bloody well she has."

"Do I?"

Ned felt the heat of anger creeping up the back of his neck. Sol's accusation was completely beyond the pale.

"If you have something more to say, say it now, Rockefeller."

Sol plunked his glass on a table and stood. He stepped toward the fireplace then turned on Ned and posed in a belligerent stance. "The jewels were in the copper tub. You saw them. I saw them."

Ned nodded.

Sol looked around to make sure they were not being heard. "Katerina had fainted on the settee. You and I pulled down the curtain to cover her."

"Yes, right. So?"

"So, while we were doing that, where was Rue?"

"On the bench! Where I left her!" Ned's anger was about to escape his control, but he had to hear his friend out.

"Was she? Really?"

Sol took a step toward Ned and gave him the look of a man who knew he'd just solved the mysteries of the universe.

"Or was she helping herself to the *Stones of Saqqarah*?"

Chapter Twelve

Her entire world was in a complete shambles.

A full day after the debacle at the ball, Rue still had no idea what she'd done. Or said. Or implied. Or failed to do. Or failed to say. It was impossible to know, and these stiff-lipped British were impossible to understand.

The note she held in her hand now confused her even more.

Lady Eugenia Strothfield will not
be entertaining Miss Rusilla Charkova
this afternoon

Rue hadn't been particularly excited about the lawn party at Lady Strothfield's, but she had intended to go. The invitation had been issued and accepted four days earlier, but now it was being rescinded? Had the event been cancelled? Or had she been uninvited?

Images of her encounter with Lady Eugenia and the girl's grandmother at the Devington ball plunged about in her mind, convincing her that it was true, that she had been uninvited.

It seemed just plain mean.

As she considered the etiquette for responding to an *uninvitation*, Del appeared at her door.

She'd been crying.

"Mother's making me go," she whispered before stepping into Rue's bedroom. "I don't want to go."

She stomped to the bed and flopped down on her stomach upon the counterpane. "I promise I won't have any fun, Rue! No fun at all!" She sobbed into her hands, shaking her pretty curls and looking completely forlorn.

"What iss wrong, my friend?"

Rue slipped to the bed and laid a hand on Del's trembling back.

"It won't be any fun if you're not there, Rue. Really it won't."

Rue leaned away.

So it was true. The lawn party was on. For everyone but Rue, it appeared. And everyone seemed to know it.

"Delfinia Wayburton, sit up now. You crush you crinoline."

Rue gave Del a supporting hand as her friend squirmed around to sit up.

"Now you tell Rue what I do, eh? What I do make them big angry?"

"N-nothing, Rue, really. They're just a bunch of sour biddies."

"No. No. Iss not true." Rue took a deep breath. "Well, maybe true, but—"

Del gave her a startled look and they both gave in to laughter.

When the moment passed, Rue continued.

"I must to know, my Del," she urged softly. "Tell me what I do wrong?"

Del gave her a sheepish look.

"Well, first of all, that little twit Eugenia has been chasing the Duke of Wellbury mercilessly for months."

"Chasing my Ned? Like running?"

"No, Rue, like mooning over—"

"Mooning? How iss mooning?"

"Oh, Rue, try to understand. She's in love with Ned Danton! She wants to marry Ned Danton. Her family *expects* her to marry Ned Danton. And *you* got in the way!"

Rue gasped. That made a great deal of sense. Eugenia was love-struck. Poor girl.

"Tell me what iss this mooning?"

Del posed herself like a pining damsel with big, soulful eyes and batted her eyelashes.

Now they both collapsed in laughter once again.

As the import of what Del had shared began to sink in, Rue knew she needed more information.

"This cannot be why they tell me not come today," she said soberly. "Iss not reason for *that*," she said, stabbing an accusatory finger toward the offending disinvitation.

"Oh," Del said, looking wary. "That."

"Yes *that*, my friend. Why they send *that*?"

"Well. You remember when you were at the refreshment table."

"Mm-hm."

"They say you coughed and the dowager offered you water."

"Mm-hm."

"And then she introduced her granddaughter."

"Mm-hm."

"And you said…"

Del paused, looking at Rue from beneath hooded eyelids.

"And I say yes, I know her little twit."

Del was silent.

"What? *That* is what I do?" Now Rue was truly confused.

"You called the granddaughter of the dowager Countess of Mecklenhold a little twit."

"Yes? So?"

Del's face sank. "Rue, darling friend, you can't do that! It's just too…rude!"

"*Twit* iss rude?" Rue felt a mass of unease begin to churn in her stomach. "Del. What means twit?"

Del shook her head sadly, placed both her hands on Rue's shoulders, and looked her squarely in the eye. "The reason you have been told not to attend the lawn party today is because you insulted Lady Eugenia so terribly that nobody will speak to you."

She took a long breath.

"Because when you called Lady Eugenia a little twit, Rue, you called her an empty-headed idiot."

~~~

Damn the *Stones of Saqqarah*! Hadn't they put that disaster behind them?

Ned found himself being drawn once again into Georgi's drama, and he resented it mightily. But she'd been his friend longer than he could remember, and he would not turn her away when she came to him with her shocking request.

He was still reeling from her announcement that she'd be going with the diplomatic envoy to Egypt.

"What exactly did the Queen ask of you?"

"She expects me to take her matched pair of ghost tigers—"

"Forgive my ignorance, Georgi, but what the devil is a ghost tiger?"

"A white tiger, Neddie. With stripes so pale they only show up in certain light. They're very rare, and I'll be taking them to the Pasha as a gift of remorse for having lost the *Stones of Saqqarah*—"

"—which have been lost for more than three hundred years, Georgi. A theft which had absolutely nothing to do with you. Or really England, for that matter."

"I know. But...but she hopes the gift will convince the Pasha not to cancel the cotton trade agreement which he has threatened to do in retaliation. The Queen is livid, Neddie. Absolutely livid."

"Oh for pity's sake, Georgi. Politics? She'd put your life in danger over politics?"

"Sol is going with us, too, Neddie. He'll be my protector. And you'll be there. I'll be as safe as a babe in the nursery."

"Then I don't understand why I must be there."

"Because you'll be there for the Suez Canal opening so you may as well spend the following week with us wooing the Pasha. We're to extend her apology in every possible way and she wants you to take the lead."

"Me? Lead the Queen's great apology tour? Why the bloody hell would she ask *me*?"

Georgi fidgeted. "I. Well. I might have suggested it."

"Georgi!"

"Oh, Neddie, I know it's a terrible thing to ask, but honestly, the Queen wouldn't take no for an answer."

Ned turned away but she darted in front of him.

"Really, Ned. I tried. I really did."

"No. I want no more to do with this, and I'll already be away two weeks. Three is just more than I can —"

Georgi quietly straightened, dropped her eyelids with a bit more fluttering of her eyelashes than absolutely necessary, and dropped a low curtsy.

"As you wish, Your Grace."

"Aw, Georgi, I—"

"Don't trouble yourself, my lord. I'm sure the old fogeys will manage to keep from embarrassing the Queen. Somehow."

Georgi began to turn slowly toward the door.

Ned paced to the window, then to the sideboard where he downed a glass of port. He wanted nothing to do with this ill-conceived adventure that had already threatened the one person he loved most in the world. But all Georgi was asking was an extra week in Egypt. No doubt at his own expense. Sol Rockefeller had depleted all his available cash, and Lord Rathmore's obsession had bankrupted Georgi's family. He'd be an idiot to think anybody but himself would foot the bill.

He knew Georgi was surviving on the goodness of her relatives at the moment. And barely more than a pittance from the Queen. But while Queen Victoria expected Georgi to soften the blow of having lost the jewels, the most she had actually offered the delegation was passage on a ship. And two fancy tigers. It was up to Georgi and Sol to manage the rest.

And they had turned to Ned.

Bloody hell.

They needed him.

"So we stay an extra week in Egypt just to engage in this bit of folly?"

Georgi's eyes slid away from his.

"Not exactly."

Her hesitation put Ned on alert. "We're not staying a week longer?"

"We, ahem, we're going a week early. To put the Pasha in a kindly frame of mind, you see. Before the Suez thing."

"The week before."

"Yes."

"And when do we leave, if I may be so bold as to ask?"

"In three days."

Ned clamped his jaws down hard on the words that threatened to escape.

"Three days. I'm to clear my diary and be ready to leave for Egypt in three days."

Georgi began to protest. "It's plenty of time to—"

"Not another word." He heaved a disgruntled sigh. "I'll do it, on one condition."

"Anything!"

"The moment you return you'll say your goodbyes and leave for America with Rockefeller."

He stepped to her and took both her hands in his, forcing her to look him in the eye. "I'll stake him to a new start. If that's what the both of you want. Those are my terms, Georgi."

He watched her bite her lip and wondered why she felt the need to pause and consider his terms. But a moment later he saw acceptance skate across her big brown eyes in a burst of joy.

"We accept!"

She threw her arms around his neck and gave him a crushing hug. "Thank you, Neddie! Oh, thank you! You won't regret it, I promise!"

Ned allowed her a prolonged hug, still wondering if he'd made a terrible mistake. But the kingpin of the jewel thieves was dead now. Kablukov could do Rue no more harm. And his henchman, Devan Maclyn, was safely ensconced in Newgate. With Sol on one side of Georgi and himself on the other, Georgi would be safe, as well.

He himself had seen the article a week ago that revealed to the world details about the original mission. It had been made clear in the article that no trace of the gems had been found. Ned had felt smug, still certain they lay hidden in the sewer pipes beneath *Rosehaven*. Now his stomach churned knowing just how wrong he'd been.

He wasn't fool enough to think the Egyptian Pasha would settle for a couple of rare beasts, but perhaps it would soften the man's anger for a while. Ned was counting on it.

~~~

Rue stepped carefully along the stone walk that led through Dowager Countess of Mecklenhold's side garden. The fragrances practically overwhelmed her senses, though perhaps it was her mission that kept her feeling lightheaded.

She had to apologize. She simply couldn't let them believe she had meant to deliver such an insult to the dowager's granddaughter. It cast too much shame on both her and her mother to let the misunderstanding go without apology.

Loose pebbles pressed cruelly into the soles of her half-boots, as if already administering punishment for her transgression. Each offending lump deepened her vow to never again speak a word if she was not absolutely certain she knew the exact meaning conveyed by each and every word that rolled off her tongue.

Voices from the terrace filtered into the quiet side garden. Laughter, chatter—all the usual sounds of young girls pitching heartily into games of croquet or lawn tennis could be heard. Rue felt for the next stepping stone with the toe of her boot. That step would take her around the corner and within sight of those who gathered on the eastern edge of the terrace.

Courage, she told herself. But it was more than courage she needed. It was old-fashioned *pluck* that was called for today.

Perhaps if she just sneaked a peek—

As slowly as she could, Rue leaned forward until she could see past the wall. It was a familiar scene. Young ladies milled about in small groups here and there, while others were engaged in genteel sport. Twice she thought she saw Del, but when the girl turned so Rue could see her face, it was someone else.

She slowly realized she knew nobody.

Maybe that would be easier, apologizing to a group of virtual strangers.

Rue squared her shoulders and stepped boldly into the mansion's grand rear garden. At the same moment, Eugenia stepped out from beneath a canopy and began walking toward the house. On Rue's other side, the dowager countess stepped out of the house and onto the terrace. Now Rue was directly between the two, as if she were the target in some medieval duel. Only nobody wore armor. Here it would be crinoline at ten paces.

The outlandish thought brought a spontaneous bubble of nervous laughter out of nowhere. As it gushed from her lips, the dowager stopped, mouth ajar and eyes bulging.

"My lady, I—" Rue choked. She absolutely had to swallow her mirth and adopt an attitude appropriate for apology.

The dowager countess stood two steps above Rue now, frozen in her surprise and batting not an eyelash. Rue cast her eyes to the right just as Eugenia came to a stop two paces from her, the girl's eyes wide as saucers.

"My ladies, my words...that is, what I saying..." Rue stumbled over her tongue as her English skittered away and she was completely unable to form the simplest thought. "Sorry iss what I—"

Her head whipped back and forth as she strove to communicate her apology. But before she could assemble the words, Lady Mecklenhold made a regal turn with her head high, shoulders stiff, and gave Rue her back. In a perfectly choreographed move, Eugenia stepped past Rue, blatantly brushing her shoulder against Rue's arm and forcing her to stumble backwards. As Rue tripped, her own arm flew forward.

Though she had not laid a finger on the girl, Eugenia grabbed her elbow and shrieked.

"She *pushed* me!"

Lady Eugenia's cry was overloud, overdramatic, completely overdone. Rue watched her make a clumsy lurch to the side, as if Rue had actually touched her, which of course she had not.

As the girl reached her grandmother, the woman put an arm around her, protecting her from the evil interloper to whom they both now showed their backsides.

"Burton," the lady growled to her butler, and flicked her head angrily back towards Rue.

The Mecklenhold butler stepped past the women and towered over Rue, his hands locked behind his back. "I will show you out, miss," he intoned.

Rue's breathing came in frightful gasps. They had given her the cut direct. And worse.

"My ladies, you must to know I not understand—"

"Go back to Russia where you belong."

The old woman's growl was so laced with meanness that Rue could do nothing but gape. All about, her the guests stood in complete silence, stunned at this unseemly display.

This moment of extreme unease was the exact moment Del and Hari burst onto the terrace.

"What is going on here?"

Hari danced prettily across the terrace and skipped part of the way down the steps.

"I make apologize, but—" Rue fought tears that sprang from her embarrassment.

Hari turned her sweetest smile on the outraged dowager.

"Oh, my lady, how very nice of Miss Charkova to beg your forgiveness," she cooed as she stopped before Lady Mecklenhold. "It was all a dreadful misunderstanding, you see. Translations can be so tricky, don't you agree?" She looked out over the gathering. "Lovely party, I dare say."

Before she moved toward Rue she gave Lady Mecklenhold a brief, untidy, absent-minded curtsy.

"Come, Rue, I've been looking all over for you. Do say you'll come with us to Buckingham tomorrow. Tea with Lady Belmont's daughters. Again!" She laughed merrily as she greeted Rue.

It was no ruse. Hari often took tea at Buckingham Palace. It was a requirement of her mother's station in the palace court.

There was little doubt that Hari, Rue, and Del were the only three present at the lawn party who had a standing invitation to tea at the palace. One could practically feel the tentacles of envy clawing at their backs as Hari swept down the steps, joined by Del, and the two looped arms with Rue. In seconds they had whisked her back around the corner of the house and out to the street, where they adjusted their gait and began walking Rue back to the Wayburton residence.

"Pay them no mind."

"They don't deserve your apology."

"Thank heaven you found me and explained about the twit," Hari gushed to Del, then turned her face toward Rue. "We were boycotting the party, you see, but when Del explained how terribly you felt about it all, well, we were going to attend the party and speak in your behalf. As it happens, we were almost too late!"

"Did you see how Eugenia faked it when she pretended you pushed her?"

"Outrageous."

"Ridiculous."

"So very childish!"

Rue walked along silently between her friends, somewhat soothed by their outrage. But as they reached the second street crossing, her heart began to stutter. They would be walking directly past Ned's town house. A smile began to form at the edge of her lips. Perhaps he would see her from a window. Perhaps he would rush into the street to greet her. She would accept his greeting and give him her prettiest curtsy. Then she would smile with a bit of regret as propriety would force her to walk on.

And she would. With her daintiest step and an oh-so-discreet swish of her sash. How she wished she had brought her parasol. She might twirl it in that flirtatious way she'd seen other women do.

The smile crept fully across her face and froze.

Ned stood on the front step of his town house.

With Lady Georgiana in his arms.

As Rue watched in horror, Ned bent to kiss her cheek. Right there on the street.

Then he slipped his arm around her waist and moved with her to the waiting carriage. When she was inside and he had closed the carriage door, Georgi reached a hand through the curtained window to cup his cheek with her gloved palm.

Blackness crept up behind Rue's eyelids, but she fought it away and maneuvered the girls in a turn that would take them prematurely across the avenue and away from Wellbury Place.

Her world was crumbling, brick by brick, and as it began to crush her, she did the only thing she could do.

She walked on.

Chapter Thirteen

"Rusilla, my pet, iss wonderful news!"

Rue's mother swept into her bedroom and sat opposite Rue, plumping her skirts as she always did to ensure she made the most elegant picture possible for anyone who might look her way. It was her habit, one that never failed to make Rue smile. Her mother was prone to drama, and it made life fun.

But not today. It seemed nothing in the world would ever make Rue smile again. It had been two days since she'd witnessed Ned kissing Georgi on his front step. He hadn't called on her or sent round a note. His last tussie mussie had long since wilted. And he hadn't attended dinner at the Marquess of Holborn's as she had expected him to. She'd been stuck through dinner between a doddering count who continually nodded off and a brash, egotistical lout just home from Cambridge.

"Hello, *mamochka*. What news?"

"Count Orlovsky has declared his intent."

Rue's stomach soured at mention of the man. *Orlovsky*. The white-haired rabbit who had chased her and her mother about Odessa for most of the previous year. Leaving him behind in

Russia had been an extraordinary relief. In the face of her grief over her father's death, the stress of keeping a serene smile on her face and cutting words from her lips when in his presence had been excruciating. For that reason alone she had been more than thrilled to put her back to him and make the trek to London. The past six weeks not having to think of the man had been sheer heaven.

But she couldn't think of the man now. It was a boon, however, that her mother didn't seem to care about her horrid behavior toward the dowager countess. That was a blessing. It was a shoulder to cry on that Rue was in need of. And an explanation of how to deal with a half dozen rescinded invitations.

"*Mamochka*, I need tell you—"

Her mother put up a hand to stop her.

"Orlovsky is ready to marry, my darling girl. Oh, this is our happy day!"

"Marry?"

"Listen!" Her mother raised the letter she had been smoothing in her lap, skimmed down the page a bit, and began to read.

> *As June is a most propitious month for nuptials,*
> *I shall hire all necessary event managers to*
> *prepare for the wedding on June 24th.*
> *I know you will approve that I have engaged*
> *the Peterhof.*

Katerina dropped the letter to her lap.

"The Peterhof! Just imagine, Rusilla. A wedding in the Winter Palace!"

She snatched the letter back up, her eyes glazed over with a joy Rue did not yet understand.

In your absence, my man will oversee arrangements. Please arrive by June 10ᵗʰ for the two weeks of festivities which shall be planned prior to the event. Four thousand rubles is the agreed upon bride gift. I shall advance additional funds for your travel. Madame Charkova, you have made this miserable man the happiest of souls.

Rue choked. She'd been listening with half an ear. But now the words her mother read began to come clear. She slipped off her chair and knelt beside her mother whose face was still aglow. It hurt Rue's heart to see her mother's great pleasure in receiving a marriage proposal less than two years after her dear husband's death. But it clearly made her mother happy, so Rue would be happy, as well.

"*Mamochka,* you will be most beautiful bride ever." She laid her head in her mother's lap and relished the feel of her mother's fingers twining in her curls.

"Rusilla, my pretty flower." Her mother's voice dropped to a whisper, followed by a long silence. "Darling?"

Her mother's hand slipped beneath Rue's cheek and lifted her face.

Rue looked into her mother's eyes, surprised to see what appeared to be compassion there. Perhaps she, too, realized it was too soon for Rue to be pleased to have another man step into her father's shoes. To honor another man as she had once honored her father.

Katerina drew her finger along the curve of Rue's cheek.

"Count Orlovsky has been most generous to arrange for the wedding, my darling girl." Her gentle fingers worked an errant curl back into its place. "But iss not me he wishes to marry."

Rue leaned away, mystified.

"I not understand, *mamochka.*"

"We will go to St. Petersburg, my flower. I have make arrangements to travel. To Berlin, then to Minsk, then to St. Petersburg. We leave in one fortnight."

Rue gasped. "Two weeks? I cannot! *Mamochka,* do not think it!"

"You must, my flower. We wait longer, we miss your wedding."

Chapter Fourteen

This was his last night before leaving with the diplomatic envoy to Egypt. Ned had more to do than the brief hours left to him would allow. And now he had to deal with this unexpected visitor.

Ned drew a calming breath and watched Rue's mother carefully. When she'd arrived at his door, Ned had been immediately alarmed for Rue's health or safety. Katerina Charkova seemed agitated, her hands fluttering oddly as she spoke.

Her beauty didn't register with him at first, but as she spoke, he came to realize what had made her daughter so appealing to him. Madam Charkova's large, limpid, brown eyes and impossibly long lashes seemed to speak more loudly than her soft, cultured voice. Every movement seemed born of grace and refinement as she moved into the room.

But there was one striking difference. Where her daughter embodied warmth, kindness, and welcome, the mother seemed cool, flinty, even aloof. And somewhat prone to drama, he was discovering.

"I do not wish to intrude, Your Grace, but iss most important

I speak with you."

"No intrusion at all, madam. I'm delighted to see you looking so well. And your daughter? She's well?"

Madam Charkova slipped off her gloves as she swept past him to take the seat he offered.

"As well as can be, I think."

The worry in her voice was impossible to miss, and Ned felt a twinge of guilt. He'd sent tussie mussies and notes to Rue every day, but in truth he'd been distracted by the business of organizing funds for what he now thought of as the great apology tour and hadn't seen Rue for three days. Three days that seemed like an eternity, but there had been no way to avoid it.

He'd set upon a sale at Tattersall's as the quickest way to manage the matter of finances. He regularly brought stock to the sale, so there would be nothing at all unusual about his appearance there. That had meant a trip to the country to determine which of his horses to sell. With all the fuss, he'd neglected his social obligations. And what pained him most, he'd neglected Rue.

The image of his beautiful Russian butter knife was always with him. With ease he could bring to mind her laugh, the toss of her curls, the feel of her hand on his arm whenever he felt need of it. Tonight he would make it up to her by monopolizing her at the Sheridan fête. She hadn't told him specifically that she would attend, but she'd purchased her costume the moment she'd heard of the event. She'd told him so in eager, glowing terms, tantalizing him with more detail than a man ought to hear.

He listened more intently to her mother now, shamed by what might be seen as his lack of attentiveness to Rue. But the woman's thoughts seemed scattered, and it took a few minutes before Ned realized Rue's mother wasn't just concerned about social trivia. Madam Charkova feared for her daughter's happiness.

Over a glass of sherry she launched into a rambling account of several women speaking badly of her daughter.

"Her sadness breaks this mother's heart. How she does miss our homeland. No Russian woman would dare to speak of her as these ladies of the *ton* have done."

"They mean nothing by it, Madam Charkova. I'm sure they're simply unused to having someone as spirited as Rusilla in their midst."

The distraught lady speared him with a look of incredulous affront.

"Spirited? I would not mind spirited. But they call her ruffian. Barbarian. Upstart. Vulgar low-bred peasant! These words drive the dagger into my heart!"

Now she began to weep.

Though Ned had at first been inclined to dismiss Madam Charkova's fears, her last words unleashed anger in him.

Confounded chinwags.

Every word they spewed was vile tittle-tattle.

They clearly didn't know Rue if they believed even half of what her mother repeated. But what mattered was that Rue's mother was sorely hurt by it.

"They cast her out, Your Grace. They keep my Rusilla from their drawing rooms, their ballrooms. They shun her!"

Ned sought words that might calm Rue's mother. In her agitated state, she seemed to be exaggerating liberally.

"Whatever it is, they'll forget about it soon, Madam Charkova. Truly, they will."

"*Nyet!*" Her hand cut the air. "They ruin my daughter. Break her spirit. This is never to happen in our homeland. She iss crying all day with worry that London does not want her." The distraught woman sniffed behind the handkerchief she held dramatically to her lips.

Ned rose and walked to the fireplace. He watched the low flame as it darted hither and yon across a fresh log.

"This will change, Madam Charkova. I'll see to that." He braced a hand against the mantel, wanting to allay her fears but not knowing what more he could say.

The woman rose and stepped a short distance away.

"No, Your Grace. It will not."

She sighed.

"My daughter must give up this fantasy that she makes her home here. They laugh at her speech. They laugh at perfect Slavic manners. They sneer at her music." She huffed. "These things they already do." She dabbed at her eyes with the handkerchief. "And they try to kill her! To kill *me!* When we do nothing!"

Madam Charkova paused, nearly overcome.

"She deserves better, Your Grace. She iss breath of spring in this cold, wet city. She iss heart of my heart. She has a smile for every person." Now the lady turned to him. "But they take that from her! They steal her smile. They break her heart."

Ned was startled to hear the woman's lovely command of the English language slip as she became more emotional. Katerina Charkova paused, then went on in a rush of words.

"She iss Russian darling, like Russian princess. All of St. Petersburg wish to dance with my Rusilla. Even Czar Alexander seat her at his table. Iss true! In Russia she lives life not even Queen of England can. But here? Here she not even get through door!" Her voice broke. "How long you watch this before you, too, step away? Hm? How long you see her weep before you cannot wish to see more tears? You will be as miserable as my Rusilla. But in Ukraine, Your Grace, in our homeland, she will not be miserable. She will be like princess."

Madame Charkova stepped toward Ned and placed a hand on his shoulder. "She trust you, Your Grace. So iss for you to do this."

Ned clenched his teeth until his jaw begged for release.

"It's for me to do what?" he asked, hoping with all his heart that she wouldn't answer.

But she did.

"Iss for you to tell her go home."

~~~

Ned was hardly aware the woman had left. Each word she had spoken weighed heavily upon him. No matter how cleverly he formed his argument, he was unable to dispel her words. Because she was right. Rusilla deserved the life of an adored princess. It had never occurred to him she came from the sort of privilege that would find her seated at the czar's table. She'd never flaunted it, or flung it before her like some path of privilege.

But could he let her go?

His heart shouted the answer before his mind even finished the question.

No. He couldn't.

With greater than usual care, Ned dressed for the Sheridan fête. It felt odd to leave the town house in a lambskin vest over a billowing peasant shirt, with leather knee-breeches that fit almost as snugly as his riding breeches. But it was a fête. And he would dress as expected.

He would do that for Rue.

He would watch her cheeks flush pink with the compliments he would lavish upon her as they danced. He would draw her into conversation in small groupings of nobles and gentry, giving them a true picture of her charming self. They would see what a gift it was to have her spirited presence among them. He would secure her promise that she would wait for him to return from Egypt.

The very last thing he would do is tell her to go back to Russia.

A throng of ideas still vied for his attention as Ned reined in his horse at Sheridan's "London cottage". Sheridan himself called it a cottage when he boasted of how he would transform his gilded home into Puk's forest glade for his annual fête. *Midsummer Night's Dream* was the theme his wife had chosen for this year's extravaganza. Sheridan had announced the fact early and often, discouraging anyone of the *ton* from even thinking of using the theme this Season.

Tonight, girls cavorted about Sheridan's lawn in gauzy gowns with small wings fluttering from their shoulders. On a lavish vine-covered stage, Oberon, king of the fairies, argued theatrically with his queen Titania.

Rusilla must be loving this.

She was *made* for a night like this. He could only hope the teasing notes he'd sent had her as laced with anticipation as he felt. Ned already had a vision of what she might look like in her own flowing costume, with colorful ribbons cascading from her hair as she danced. He cast a look about the grounds as he wandered, hoping to spy the place that would have drawn Rue. By the time he had made the rounds, he'd become convinced she had not yet arrived. He chuckled. She had no need of the grand entrance she must be planning. Every time she stepped into a room was grand.

The small pouch of coins he'd brought jingled softly in his vest pocket as he walked. The sound redirected his feet to the interior of the house. He scarcely recognized the place with so many leafless trees lining the foyer. Each tree was liberally draped with ribbons and flowing scarves, providing private alcoves for trysting couples. Beyond the foyer, a faux woodland path led to the gaming room, where fellows dressed in varying degrees of elfin gentry already gathered.

Ned stepped to the doorway and surveyed the tables. A hand beckoning from the far corner drew him in.

"We've a spare chair, Danton," the man called. Ned recognized the voice of the Earl of Delriven and walked in his direction. "Glad to see you've rid yourself of the little gypsy," the earl bellowed.

Around the room men here and there beat a hand against their own tables, offering their agreement, though none of them looked in his direction.

Heat flared at the back of his neck, but he continued to the earl's table.

"Gentlemen."

He greeted the group as pleasantly as he could after their rudeness. They'd all had one or two tongue-loosening brandies, and he was willing to overlook it. He drew back a chair and sat.

"What are we playing," he asked amiably.

"Shoot the Russian," the Marquess of Strothfield laughed.

Several of the men seated at his table chuckled.

"Charkova Ruse," another sniggered. "That's what we're playing. Charkova Ruse!"

Ned bit back the swift rejoinder that had sprung to his lips and swept up the cards that had just been dealt him. "Looks like you're playing Pharo. I'm in," he said quietly as he laid a few coins on the table. But he couldn't help offering the Marquess of Strothfield a lingering look of disapproval.

"Let's play to a gypsy draw," the marquess smiled.

Now Ned was truly irked. The man just would not let it go. Had they all been infected by their wives' wagging tongues? Is this what Madam Charkova had been trying to explain?

The heat on his neck swelled to a blistering flame that crawled around his collar, threatening to enflame his cheeks. Ned dropped his cards to the table and drew back.

"Now, now, calm yourself, Danton. It's no shame for a young duke to be drawn in by the likes of her." The marquess grinned. "Happens to the best of us."

Ned seethed. "What exactly do you mean by 'the likes of her'?" he asked.

"Nothing at all, Danton. Nothing at all. Just glad to see you quit of the little twit, that's all."

For some reason that sparked uproarious laughter.

Ned shoved his chair back and stood. "You'll kindly refer to Miss Charkova in the manner she deserves, sir."

He was furious. A bit of ribbing was one thing, but this vitriol was completely unacceptable.

"*She* deserves? You're concerned about what *she* deserves?" Now Strothfield dropped his own cards. "It's a shame you didn't teach Miss Charkova that bit of etiquette."

Ned stepped around the table and lowered his voice. "Explain yourself."

He heard the challenge in his own voice and couldn't regret it.

"Don't tell me you haven't heard," the marquess sneered.

Ned gritted his teeth. "Suppose you enlighten me."

Strothfield stood, all pleasantness dropping away from his face.

"That low-life little gypsy came onto *my* grounds, on *my* estate, and called *my* daughter a little twit. But we've taken care of it, Danton. You needn't worry yourself about it. She won't be showing her face here again." He gestured toward the men at his table. "Or anywhere, for that matter."

The marquess resumed his seat, leaving Ned reeling.

This is what her mother had been speaking of. One innocent slip of a word she didn't understand—a word to which he himself had introduced her—and she was now being completely shunned.

And it was his fault.

He stared at the back of Strothfield's head. He would fix this here and now.

"It's I who needs the lesson, my lord."

The men at the table who had begun to resume play, dropped their cards and turned toward him. The marquess merely rubbed his forehead with his hand, as if for him, the matter was over. At last he turned his face up to acknowledge Ned.

Ned felt the heat recede from his face as a coolness overtook him.

"It was I who used the word in Miss Charkova's presence. If there is anyone to blame for the use of it, blame me."

The marquess huffed. "Nobody cares how you address your staff, Your Grace. That is an entirely different matter. You may call common baggage by any name you choose."

Ned squared himself. "Then I repeat, I must beg your forgiveness, because it was not a commoner to whom I referred."

He turned and scooped up his coins.

"The little twit, sir, was your daughter."

CHAPTER FIFTEEN

RUE DROPPED HER SODDEN HANDKERCHIEF into the basket that sat beside her dressing table. She had cried for so long she was quite sure a lifetime's portion of tears had been used up.

The gorgeous lace costume she was to have worn tonight hung on her wardrobe door. Rue had looked forward to the Sheridan fête from the first moment Hari and Del had described it to her. They had gushed over the lavish decorations everyone expected—all true, they swore, because they'd heard it directly from the mousie's snout, meaning the Sheridan girl.

Rue had been all a-tingle with anticipation of the event. And now, despite her attempt to apologize, her invitation to the fête had been retracted.

She had pinned so many hopes on this night. The way Ned had attended to her throughout their past social engagements had thrilled her no end. He had eyes for her. And only her.

So tonight her tears were for Ned, whose absence of late made it abundantly clear that he had heard of her shame. She had not received a single note or even a single flower for three days. And four nights without social engagements had her climbing the walls. Now, with her crying jag beginning to abate, Rue remembered her mother's worrisome plan, and once again despair enveloped her.

It was impossible to contemplate going back to the Ukraine. And even more impossible to contemplate marriage to the old White Rabbit. Each time the thought of Count Orlovsky intruded, her stomach leaped into her throat and her heart began to pound mercilessly. The bond she felt with Ned was real. The affection was true. The fledgling love was honest. Turning away from it was unthinkable.

And yet he had turned away from her.

But it was different for him. He was a duke, with responsibilities she couldn't even fathom. He must hold his place in Society, and being associated with her could only damage his position. It was a cold, cruel fact, but one she was unable to ignore. And one that made her sob yet again until at last she beat a pillow with her fist.

She had never been a weepy maiden, and she was aghast that she'd suddenly become one. But there was a way to resolve this. She would accept the few feeble invitations that came her way for the next day or two, then pack her things and prepare to travel. She would decline Count Orlovsky's proposal of marriage and cast her net far and wide. Surely there was someone out there who could make her heart race. Someone who might measure up to Ned. Surely.

But she could never leave without exposing her true feelings to Ned. Nor could she allow Orlovsky to count on her compliance with the marriage he and her mother accepted as fact.

Rue stood and loosened the pins from her hair as she

contemplated her next task. First, she must write Orlovsky. He had already thrown far too many rubles into the marriage pot. She couldn't let him toss any more. All she needed to set that to rights was pen and paper.

Rue reached for the wardrobe door, intent upon donning the simplest gown she could find in order to descend to the library. As she did so, her hand bumped the white lace costume, making it dance merrily as it swayed on its hanger.

The sight of it made her smile. Why not? She could at least wear it just this once.

The dress slid easily on, and she was able to reach its fastening ribbons without need of assistance. In truth, it needed a more substantial underdress, but for this quick mission, she saw no need to bother.

Lady Wayburton had given most of the staff the evening off before she and Del left for the evening. It gave Rue a reckless feeling that she need not even bother with slippers.

She moved swiftly down the quiet hall and tripped lightly down the stairs. The costume flowed so perfectly she couldn't resist a small pirouette as she stepped onto the landing. But as she reached for the banister to descend further, she froze.

A man stood in the lighted foyer, clad in country leathers and a muslin shirt. His tousled hair hung loosely against his collar, an errant lock dipping rakishly across his brow. He gazed at her in startled wonder, as if she'd just slid down from the moon.

"Ahem."

The Wayburton butler cleared his throat.

"The Duke of Wellbury to see you, Miss Charkova."

He bowed and stepped out of sight.

Or perhaps he stayed. She couldn't really say, because for

Rusilla Charkova there was only one other person in the room. Her Ned.

~~~

Ned stood planted in the foyer, unable to move. The vision above him was one he would have found it impossible to describe, were he ever called upon to do so. But the vision was his and his alone. He couldn't imagine sharing something so precious with another living soul.

Rue stood like a fairy creature, poised on the landing as if painted there. He knew she was real, because her eyes flashed with welcome, her lips shaping the sweet round 'o' of surprise. He'd watched her descend from the upper staircase, her gauzy gown flowing gracefully about her. As she completed her dainty twirl, the folds of lace continued to dance above her bare feet.

No. Above her naked feet.

That was what she had called them when she shared so freely that her favorite feeling was running through the grass barefoot. He'd thought it a charming expression, but now it seemed inadequate.

Now her naked feet barely rooted her, like a butterfly about to take flight.

And yet it wasn't her feet that stole his breath, but the beautiful silhouette lighted from the back by the sconce on the wall behind her. He felt guilty looking at such an intimate scene, and yet he couldn't make himself look away. Visible through the gauzy lace, her long legs and slender torso seemed perfectly formed, perfectly shaped, perfectly—

"Your Grace? What you do here?"

Her lilting Russian accent drew him to his senses.

"I—I missed you at the Sheridan fête."

She stepped closer to the banister, into a bit of shadow, banishing the mesmerizing light that had so captivated him.

"I was not...I mean, I not like to go."

For a moment Ned puzzled over her expression. Her words said she chose not to go. Her face told a very different story. Ned stepped up onto the bottom stair, knowing he shouldn't, but unable to bear the distance between them.

"You just wanted to stay home and dance around in your costume? Is that it?"

He took another step.

"Your Grace, I—"

"Come down here now, Rusilla Charkova. Or I will come up there."

"*Nyet!*"

"Then come down here. Please."

He watched her consider, and when he backed away to the foyer floor, she began to move.

It was painful, watching her come to him and knowing he dared not run to her, sweep her into his arms and carry her into the night. But she had been shamed enough in recent days, and it was his fault. He would not add further to her burden. Nor would he take advantage of the leniency Lady Wayburton had shown him following their harrowing escape from the bowels of *Rosehaven*.

Ned turned and stepped into the drawing room. The gypsy shawl that had been carelessly draped across a high-backed chair caught his eye. He lifted it and shook out its folds as Rue entered the room. He held it out to her and she came toward him.

As she turned, he draped both ends of the shawl about her and held them together as he drew close behind her. Whether she leaned back against him or he crowded next to her, he couldn't be sure, but the feel of her again in his arms, warming his chest, flooded him with relief.

"I've missed you," he whispered into her ear.

She stiffened and moved away from him to stand by the fireplace.

"Rue?"

"Why you say this?"

Her words were such a contrast to those she had spoken when last they were together that Ned was certain he'd misunderstood. He stepped to the fireplace, but resisted his impulse to touch her.

He wanted to remind her of the letters he'd sent in the last few days, but he was suddenly embarrassed to bring to mind the scandalous loving phrases he'd penned.

"We were to meet at the fête tonight. When you weren't there, I thought something might be wrong."

She turned sharply toward him. "Tell me true, my Neddie. Not these words. Only true words!"

Ned was aghast at her emotion. She seemed wounded. Terribly hurt.

"It *is* the truth, Rue. Read my letters again. Maybe—"

"Letters?"

Now she swatted him with her hand, losing her grip on the shawl and letting it fall to the floor. The light in the stairway had been nothing compared to the way the flickering flames illuminated her. But he dared not let it distract him, because her hurt was quickly turning to anger.

"What letters! You not send letters. You just go, and I not see you. When I do see you, iss with Lady Georgiana. Iss her you kiss. Not Rue!"

She shifted away, visibly trying to calm herself.

"Go now. Iss no matter."

The force of her words stunned him as none ever had. "Rue, I wrote you three times in five days, laying out my plans and professing my—well, surely the flowers conveyed my sentiment. And the kiss you speak of? That was no more than a peck on the cheek!"

Her tears flowed freely now.

"Iss my wish to believe you, my Neddie. But I cannot."

She flung out her arms as if she could encompass the house.

"Where are these flowers you speak of, eh? And these letters? Here? No! There? No!"

The despair in her voice moved him to action. Ned reached a hand to her shoulder and brought her round to face him. He wanted to crush her to him, to let the conviction in his bones seep into her until she couldn't possibly deny the truth of his words. Instead, both his hands slipped higher to cup her face.

"Rue. Not a minute goes by that I don't want to hold you like this. To touch your face. To...to..."

Her upturned face looked so full of sorrow he could scarcely breathe. Her lower lip quivered and he could tell she fought to still it, but her body that was clearly scorched by the same emotion he felt in every fiber of his being seemed unable to do anything but lean toward him. And he could do nothing but draw her closer.

With a tenderness he'd never felt before, he touched her lips with his own. Her soft, trembling mouth launched waves of need in him, even as her answering kiss seemed to reveal her own sweet need.

He prayed her quiet moan meant she forgave him.

~~~

"I swear, Rue," he said between kisses. "I swear upon my life." He caressed her cheek. "I wrote to you. Volumes!"

"Oh my Neddie," Rue whispered. His kiss had torn away her fears and replaced them with the certainty that it was she whom he loved. His kiss that seemed born in heaven was meant for only her. Not Georgiana. But her and her alone. When he begged her to be here when he returned from Egypt, her heart soared.

"My heart miss you so, my Neddie."

Ned crushed her to him, lifting her off her feet and turning with joy as they clung to one another. "I'll never leave you, love. Never!"

His bright eyes pierced her with the truth of his words. He loved her. He wanted her. But as his eyes began to close and his lips sought hers, her heart tumbled to her feet.

"Neddie!"

She pushed away from him and stumbled. Ned reached a hand to steady her, but she held out her arm stiffly, warning him to keep his distance.

"Rue? What is it?"

Ned stood two steps away from her, breathing heavily into the air they'd warmed only a moment ago.

"Oh Neddie," she wailed. "Iss such big trouble!"

Now Ned laughed. "You scared me there for a minute, Rusilla

Charkova." He took a step toward her. "Don't be doing th—"

"No! I must think!"

He laughed again. "Sweetheart, thinking is the very last thing you need to do right now. Come here."

He reached for her hand but she flung it behind her back.

"No, Neddie! I must think what to do."

"It's not so difficult, Rue. Just say you love me as much as I love you, and the rest of the world can figure out how to deal with it."

The tear that had trembled on her lower lid slid down her cheek. It seemed to blaze a trail that would be impossible to erase. She loved Ned, and was desperate to believe his words, now that his tantalizing kisses had given them some bit of credence. He'd been absent through her crushing days of banishment by the *ton*, but he'd come to her tonight. He'd sought her out. Was it possible that she could make her life here with him? That her mother could smooth things over with Orlovsky? Would her mother ever forgive her if she did not return to Russia?

These thoughts seemed to tangle themselves into a web of doubt, casting darkness over the bright joy she'd felt only moments earlier. It was time she told Ned of her mother's plans, but how?

A commotion in the foyer had them both turning toward the drawing room door at the same moment that Katerina Charkova sailed through it. She drew off her capelet as she assessed what she was seeing.

"Have you come to congratulate my daughter, Your Grace?" She tossed the short cape dramatically onto a side chair.

Ned stepped away from Rue, an odd sort of guilty confusion

washing across his face.

"What has the very talented Miss Charkova done that I should be congratulating?"

"*Mamochka!*" Rue attempted to stop her mother from speaking. "Is late hour. You very tired, yes?" She rushed to her mother's side and attempted to draw her back toward the stairs. But as they reached the doorway, Katerina stopped and turned.

"You surprise me, daughter," she smiled, then turned fully toward Ned.

"My Rusilla iss betrothed to the wealthiest man in Russia."

"But I not—" Rue was desperate to convince Ned she would stay here, that never in a million years would she marry Orlovsky, but in her state of panic, her English deserted her and only Russian words roiled in her head.

In the same moment, the front door opened once again and Lady Georgiana stepped into the foyer.

"They said I might find you here, Neddie."

~~~

Ned stood speechless in Lady Wayburton's foyer.

"What are you doing here, Georgi?"

"She has the jewels, Neddie. She has to."

Georgi stared straight at Rue, her gaze as accusing as any he'd ever witnessed. He'd known even before he asked that the answer couldn't be welcome, but this was the last thing he could have suspected.

"That's ridiculous, Georgi. She couldn't possibly—"

Georgi took a step toward him.

"You need to read this."

Ned took the paper she held out to him.

"Wh—?"

"He saw her."

"Who?"

"The Earl of Charleton."

Her last words released the tension that had been building in his chest.

"That liar? That scoundrel? Georgi, you can't believe a word—"

"Read it! He says that night in the bathing parlor you were pulling down some kind of curtain. You and Sol. And it got stuck and you had to go around to the back side and work it loose."

"Yes, we needed something to wrap around the women who were soaking wet, but—"

"That's when he saw her do it. Or heard her, rather. She went to the copper tub and recovered the stones."

Ned leaned heavily on the newel post. It seemed an impossible task to raise his head to look at Rue, but he knew he had to. Rue's mother had been unconscious on the settee that night. If Maclyn heard a woman moving to the tub, it could only be—

"Is it true?"

The look on her face nearly took him to his knees. Was it shock? Disbelief? Or guilt? He couldn't decipher it.

"*Nyet*! My Ned! I not do this thing. How you think I can do this thing?"

She flew across the room to stand before him, but to his great shame he found himself backing away.

"Is this the 'big trouble' you spoke of?"

"How you think this?"

Her voice had dropped to an incredulous whisper.

"Is this what you were trying to tell me before your mother appeared with her," he choked on the words, "her joyous news of your betrothal?"

"Yes! I try to tell you I not go!"

"What were you going to do, Rue? Sell the jewels so you could stay in London?"

"No! I not have them!" Rue rushed forward and clutched at his shirt, tears streaming down her cheeks. But his hands refused to touch her.

Georgi stepped to Ned's side.

"Maclyn put it in his confession, Neddie. It's signed. And witnessed by Sol."

"What?"

Like a painting unfolding on canvas, the moments of doubt presented themselves. The night he met Rusilla Charkova she helped to deceive Maclyn so Ned could speak with Georgi. Her acting had been flawless. When they took Georgi to the sanatorium Rue's perfect small lies deceived the doctor and his staff. Tonight when she pretended she hadn't received his letters he'd actually believed her. How many other times had she lied? Or acted a role in order to smooth the way?

It was too much. He had to think.

It broke his heart to pull her hands away from his chest, but he had to do it. He had to leave. If he was ever to look upon her again, he had to find some way he could trust her.

"Your mother's right, Rue. Perhaps it would be best if you just go home."

Without another word he turned from her and strode out into the night—away from the only woman to whom he'd every truly opened his heart.

Chapter Sixteen

THE FRONT DOOR STOOD WIDE, flung open as the duke gathered his horse and Lady Georgiana hurried to a waiting carriage. Rue watched, stunned at the crashing emotions that threatened to bring her to her knees.

Just moments ago her future had come into focus as she twirled in Ned's arms. Every question was banished with the certainty that this was where her future lay. Here. In England. With Ned.

His kiss had done that. And then in a flurry of accusations he had left her dumbfounded.

All she understood was that he had torn himself from her, tugged away by lies from the woman who had owned his heart since childhood.

Now the old doubts resurfaced. How could she believe he loved her when he'd made up his fantastical story about letters and flowers? In the days since she had last seen Ned she'd received no flowers and no letters. At best, he'd grossly exaggerated his efforts in his rush to encourage her to trust him. At worst, he'd been outright lying.

But that's what love was about, wasn't it? Trusting?

Rue stumbled to her room, too distraught to make sense of the conflicting emotions.

Her whole body felt numb as she loosened the ribbons of the lacy costume and let it drop to the floor.

"What have you done?"

Rue turned at the sound of her mother's shrill voice. Katerina rushed into the room and bent to scoop up the lace gown.

"You shame me, daughter."

It was impossible to mistake her mother's tone for anything but anger.

"I did not take the jewels, *mamochka*! You must to believe!" She drew a breath to explain, but her mother forged on.

"I don't care about the stupid jewels. You were not to go to the Sheridans, Rusilla! You promised. The sooner they forget the name Charkova the better! But you...you parade around in this! Like a strumpet showing off every indecent part of you!"

Her mother shook the gown in Rue's face as she laced her tirade with Russian words that underscored her displeasure.

Rue felt the words as if they'd been knives hurled across the room at her. Forget her name? She didn't want that. She didn't want her presence here erased. Yes, she had been treated badly, but it wasn't entirely their fault. And to make them forget they'd ever known her? She couldn't wish for that. Ever.

"*Mamochka*, I did not go." Rue grabbed the costume from her mother's hands. "I just wear it here."

"And you leave it here, *dragotsennyy*. Leave this reminder." She took back the gown from Rue and flung it into the corner. "Only think of your beautiful life to come, precious one. Now you must pack. Quick-quick. I will call the maid to help you."

Rue's eyes lingered on the pretty lace gown that lay in a heap. She wanted desperately to pick it up, to hold it near her heart, to caress the places that had been crushed by Ned's passionate embrace. And then her mother's words penetrated her reverie.

"Pack? What you say, *mamochka*?"

Her mother paused in the doorway. "Pack tonight, precious one. Our plans have at last fallen into place."

She drew a letter from her reticule and kissed the ornate seal of Count Orlovsky.

"Tomorrow morning we go to Halvord House. The next day they transport us to the channel crossing. Oh, just think, my Rusilla!" She clutched the letter to her breast. "Ten days from tomorrow we step off the train in our beloved Odessa!" She turned to leave. "And you, my *dragotsennyy*, you must not ruin it."

Katerina's face filled with joy as she blew her daughter a kiss and disappeared into the hallway.

Tomorrow? They would leave London tomorrow? And less than a fortnight later she would face Orlovsky in Odessa? No. No, no! It was too soon. Too fast.

She needed time! Time to prove to Ned that she was telling the truth. That she had no idea where the *Stones of Saqqarah* were.

The lump that had risen to her throat grew to the size of a boulder, escalating her breathing to a shallow speed that threatened to outpace her lungs.

Time was what she needed. Time to speak with Ned calmly and dispassionately. Surely her mother would understand.

Rue retrieved the lovely lace costume and hung it in the back of the wardrobe. She slipped into her dressing gown as she collected her thoughts and began to pack her trunk. It filled quickly with the garments she'd brought from Russia. But when she reached for the red gypsy shawl, her hand faltered. Everything about it launched trembling thoughts within her.

Perhaps it was the boldness of the color which inspired her sudden courage, or perhaps it was the depth of her need for time to validate her feelings for Ned. Whatever it was, the jolt of it drew Rue to her feet and sent her into the hallway. She would convince her mother to wait until after she had a chance to speak with Ned in the morning. She was certain that if they both spoke plainly and sincerely, she would know what course to take. Either he would believe her and she would forgive him for his doubt. Or—

"*Mamochka!*"

Rue sailed into her mother's room, ready to make her case to stay in London. But her mother was nowhere to be seen. Rue turned a full circle, words sitting restlessly on the tip of her tongue.

"*Mamochka?*"

Familiar gowns lay strewn across her mother's bed, some partially folded, others rather carelessly laid out. Three trunks sat by, ready to be filled with her mother's lavish wardrobe. It was twice the size of the wardrobe she'd brought from Russia. Rue's mother had taken great delight in acquiring the finest new London fashions, dreaming of the doors that would open to her as mother of Count Orlovsky's new bride. The very thought of it turned Rue's stomach.

Her mother's headdresses and jewelry were strewn across the pretty dressing table, but there was no sign of her mother.

Impatience grew to the bursting point as Rusilla pouted in

the center of the room, debating what to do. Her eye was drawn to the lady's writing desk that sat against the wall, its cover lowered to form the desktop. From the center of the room she recognized the letter her mother had waved about moments earlier. The letter from Count Orlovsky. It turned her impatience to budding anger as she swooped to the desk and snatched up the maddening missive.

As she held the letter, the happenings of recent days paraded across her mind. Yes, she had been terribly hurt by the shunning of the *ton*. But that could be fixed, couldn't it? In time, perhaps. It was this stupid letter that stood between herself and Ned. It was this letter that had committed her mother to departing for home with such haste.

"What now, precious one?" Katerina Charkova breezed into the room as if preparing to travel was her favorite pastime in the whole world.

"I cannot go, *mamochka*. Not yet." Rue set her shoulders for the battle she knew would materialize within seconds.

It began with an exasperated sound from her mother. "Iss for the best, Rusilla. You know I am right."

"I don't know that, *mamochka*. How you be so sure?"

Her mother whirled to face her. "Experience, darling! You will have every pretty thing your heart desires. Count Orlovsky has promised it!"

"Mama! I not want pretty things. I want—"

Somehow she couldn't say it.

Her mother stepped closer. "What iss it you want? Hm? You want to stay here where everybody laughs at you? Hm? You want to stay here where everyone goes to parties where you receive no invitation? No!" She dropped a pile of smallclothes into an open trunk. "My *dragotsennyy* will not be the joke!"

Katerina disappeared in a huff, leaving Rue standing among her mother's disarray.

Rue began to fold the letter from Orlovsky, but one line caught her eye. Her mother had failed to read the line aloud earlier, and now its omission—or rather, rewording—seemed stunning. Earlier her mother had read it as a bride price of ten thousand rubles. That would mean that Count Orlovsky was offering her mother a small fortune for the privilege of marrying her daughter.

But the letter didn't say *bride price*. It said *dowry*.

Rue was aghast. Where would her mother get ten thousand rubles to offer as a dowry for her daughter?

It was impossible. But more, it was humiliating, as if her mother was offering such a fortune for the old white rabbit to take an unmarriageable daughter off her hands.

With a flare of temper, she swept her hand upward, bent upon throwing the offending letter into the dustbin. But her hand froze as a horrid thought pierced her mind. It sickened her to even think it.

Was it possible?

"Oh, *mamochka*!"

She clamped her hand across her mouth to stifle the unthinkable words from spilling out.

Was it her mother who had taken the *Stones of Saqqarah*?

~~~

Rue sat on the edge of her mother's bed fingering the box that had been so poorly hidden it had taken her a scant five minutes to find it. Tears streamed from her eyes as she clutched the small packet she'd found resting within it. The box had contained no jewels, but what she saw there seemed far, far worse.

He'd been telling the truth. Ned had written her three times, just as he had insisted. But her mother had hidden his letters from her. The very thought of it was crushing. Not only had she been crushed by not hearing from him, but Rue had hurled accusations at Ned, insisting he'd lied about sending them.

Now here they were, in a pretty packet tied up with a blue ribbon. Unopened and hidden away.

How dare she betray her daughter like this, by denying Rue the words that would have validated Ned's feelings for her.

And she knew they would.

Rue slid the top envelope from beneath the ribbon. Her fingers trembled as she broke the seal and unfolded the missive. Her eyes blurred as the tears refused to abate. But slowly they adjusted and she began to read.

> *My dear Rusilla,*
> *You have not answered my recent letters, but I feel*
> *certain if I were to stand before you today you would*
> *tell me what my heart yearns to hear. And so I will*
> *tell you what my own being cannot withhold. Before*
> *you came into my life, my days had a certain color,*
> *a certain rhythm. Now that I know life with you in*
> *my world, I realize what true brilliance is, and I'm*
> *stunned to think I'd been willing to accept so much*
> *drabness, so much mediocrity in the past. I am so*
> *taken with this new state of being that I shall do all*
> *I can to convince you to stay in London, at least long*

enough for us to know if this thing we are experienc-
ing is real. Do think about it, darling Rusilla. And
do not dare to think that I shall await your reply with
any kind of patience at all.
                              Your devoted Ned.

How her heart would have soared reading those words! But tonight, with the vision of his disappointment and doubt still so fresh in her mind, his words brought only torrents of tears.

~~~

A dark tempest swirled between Rue and her mother late into the night. Denials were rampant and pleading constant as the two remained locked in verbal battle. But the letters she'd found could not be denied, and helped Rue force Katerina to give up the idea of leaving for Halvord House the next morning.

"You lie to me, *mamochka*. You steal from me." She held up the letters in her trembling hand. "You owe this daughter time to fix this terrible thing."

Rue held the deception over her mother's head until at last she agreed to stay in London—but only until the Duke of Wellbury returned from the Queen's diplomatic mission.

When at last they called a truce and descended for breakfast, they were surprised to be met in the hall by Lady Wayburton. She was on edge. Nervous. Clearly unsettled. And poor Del hung in the background, wringing her hands.

"Good morning, Rosella," Rue's mother said brightly.

She moved forward to share their usual greeting of a kiss on each cheek. But today Lady Wayburton drew away, refusing to look Katerina in the eye as she glared at Rue.

Rue was shocked at the scene, and any greeting that might spring to her lips was quickly quelled by Lady Wayburton's stern face.

"Philbert is taking your luggage to Halvord House. I wish you godspeed."

The curt statement drew gasps from Rue and her mother and a stifled wail from Del. It was Katerina who found her tongue first.

"We have decided to delay our return, my dear friend. Is it possible to delay—"

"Impossible, I'm afraid. I'm told you will be able to break your fast at Halvord House but you must make haste."

She stepped aside, clearly expecting them to take their leave.

Rue stood trembling on the stairway. Their wonderful host was turning them out? Without warning? This was dreadful. Her mind pleaded that this couldn't be so, but every word in her and her mother's defense seemed to die on her tongue.

Philbert stepped forward with their cloaks and parasols. His own face revealed a good bit of pride over his part in this debacle. Rue and her mother looked aghast at one another. Their personal paraphernalia still lay upstairs on their dressing room tables. And numerous other items had not yet made it into the trunks.

"But we haven't finished—"

"Thorndike will supervise the collection of your things which will be delivered to Halvord House by this evening. Good day."

Lady Rosella Wayburton turned and disappeared into the morning room, closing the door behind her.

"I'm so sorry!" Del began to cry as she darted across the hall to gather Rue in a crushing hug. "So sorry!"

"What iss happening, Del? Why your mother do this?"

Del reared back a bit and dropped her chin. "She...she thinks you've been hiding stolen jewels here. In our house."

"Del! Is not possible! I tell you true, I have done nothing!"

"I know! I believe you! But Lady Georgiana has poisoned Mother's mind about this and she...she..."

"She has turned us out."

The morning room door opened a crack. "Delfinia? A word."

"I'm so sorry!" Del drew close and whispered. "Stay in London as long as you can. I shall send word the moment His Grace asks after you." She hugged Rue fiercely.

"Delfinia?" Del's mother sounded even more insistent.

Del tucked a parcel wrapped in brown paper into Rue's hands and whispered, "I promise. I'll send a note every night to Halvord House."

And she disappeared into the morning room.

The horror of the scene began at last to plant its ugliness in Rue's mind. Lady Wayburton had heard about the jewels. From Philbert, no doubt. She'd believed the accusation, already confirming it with Lady Georgiana. And she was turning her guests out into the street. If she could do this, what would the rest of the world do?

Rue felt faint. She knew what they'd do. And she knew already what it would feel like to live her life shunned by a world that couldn't take the time to discover the truth. A world where Ned, too, might believe she could ever do such a thing.

She hadn't taken the jewels. And after the long night of arguing she was certain that her mother had not, either. But the only thing Society wanted was for the guilty parties to disappear.

And so they would.

CHAPTER SEVENTEEN

HALVORD HOUSE WAS A STINKY PLACE.

Every bit of wood and fabric in the building had long ago soaked up the odors from a huge tannery just six blocks away. Staying here for three weeks like Rue and her mother expected to made them feel as though the smell would be permanently imprinted on their clothing, in their hat boxes, even in the leather of their half-boots.

Once they were settled, Rue's first errand was to collect as much lavender as possible from the nearby market. She retrieved all of her handkerchiefs and tied them full of the pretty, sweet-smelling sprigs. It was a soothing task to twist and tie the handkerchiefs into small sachets. And when she was done, she tucked the sachets into each layer of clothing in their several trunks. She smoothed out the fabrics, adjusted the hat feathers so they weren't crushed, and closed the trunks and boxes back up.

She had just climbed onto a chair to retrieve the last of the hatboxes her mother kept on top of the wardrobe when her mother breezed into the room.

"What are you doing!"

Her mother's alarmed cry startled Rue, and she nearly lost her balance. The hatbox teetered and was about to fall to the floor but she grabbed it just as it began to tumble.

"Rusilla! Give it to me!"

Rue sought a calmer voice. "Iss alright, *mamochka*. I put good smells in our trunks. You like?" She held out the impromptu sachet she was about to put into the last hatbox. But it only agitated her mother.

"*Bozhe moy!* Not in that one, daughter. Here. Give it to me."

Her mother lurched close to the chair Rue balanced upon and made a grab for the hatbox Rue held. Rue knew it was her mother's favorite. Her mother had personally carried it everywhere they went in the last few days. But as she grabbed for the hatbox, its leather strap caught on Rue's wrist.

"Stop, *mamochka*! Wait!"

In her agitation, Katerina kept pulling, and with her final jerk the hatbox, Rue, and her mother all tumbled to the floor.

"Ack! *Mamochka*!"

Arms and legs and hat feathers landed in a tangled heap.

"Oh Mama. Vat you do now?"

Rue rolled to the side to pull away a small rock that was pressing against her ribs, and the breath left her lungs in a startled whoosh. What came away in her hand was not a rock. It was a polished oval emerald as long as a baby's fist.

There was no moment of wonder, no sudden realization of what her mother had done. Just the pitiful despair of knowing what she'd suspected but refused to admit.

Her mother had stolen the *Stones of Saqqarah*. And she'd been carrying them around in a hatbox.

"How could you?"

Rue could summon little more than a whisper, but it gained her mother's attention. She should have found some satisfaction in her mother's guilty face when she saw what was in Rue's hand. But it was too little and too late.

"You lie to me. All these many days, you lie." Rue held out the glittering stone and her mother at least had the grace to shrink from it.

"Rusilla, my daughter, you must understand."

"Understand? Iss no understand. You steal these. And you let them think it was me. Me! Your daughter!"

"Rue, my precious one, I just took them, and then once I had them I...I didn't know what to do. And then..."

"Stop. I cannot hear this." Rue grabbed a large diamond her mother had found lying between them. "Give them to me." She turned and began to search for the rest.

"No! These are your dowry!"

Rue turned to her mother, seething with an anger she had never felt before. "I have no need of dowry, *mamochka*. I not to marry White Rabbit Orlovsky. I tell you so many time, why you not hear this daughter?" Rue sighed and shook her head. "I will return these. And if you try to stop me I—"

"You'll what, daughter? You'll see me in prison? Is this what you want?"

Rue couldn't speak.

"Then do it. Put me in prison. It will clear your name if that is what you must do." Katerina began to scramble around collecting the remaining diamonds. The second large emerald eluded them until they realized it had never spilled from the hatbox.

"We are ready now, daughter. We have them all. Come. We

will go to the constable."

"Mama! Stop. I need to think."

"No thinking. Just doing. I am ready."

In her typical dramatic fashion, Katerina drew herself up from the floor, adjusted her clothing, set her hat upon her head and turned toward the door like a prisoner heroically facing the chopping block.

"*Mamochka*. Stop. You not go to prison." Rue retrieved a square of brown paper from the table and placed the priceless gemstones in the center of it. "I return them. Somehow."

And somehow she would. But not now. Now she had to think.

Rue tied up the packet with a length of string and sent her mother down for tea. She had to be alone. She had to figure this out. She had to be free of these jewels which sought yet again to ruin her life.

~~~

It was just a half-formed idea, but somehow she had to make it work.

Rue walked across the boulevard where Del and Hari waited for her in front of the Egyptian Consulate at Chesterfield Gardens. Her stomach churned with worry. Already she was having doubts about her plan.

It had seemed so simple. Three innocent young ladies visiting the consulate's museum and stopping for a cup of rich, dark Egyptian coffee in the small tea room.

In her mind's eye, Rue had envisioned eluding the girls for a moment, dropping her packet of jewels in an inconspicuous place, and leaving. Then she'd write an anonymous letter telling them where to look.

Why wouldn't it work?

Rue clutched the packet she'd wrapped in brown paper and tied up with string. Traffic shifted and Rue skipped the last few steps up onto the walkway, keeping her distance from an elderly woman who was hurrying down the consulate's front steps.

"Rue! We've been so worried about you!" Hari drew Rue into a fierce hug.

"Are you alright?" Del's whispered concern warmed Rue's heart. They still cared for her.

"I fine. You beautiful to come here for me!"

"We've been so eager to see you we wouldn't miss it for the world!"

"Come, girls! I've arranged for a tour!"

Rue turned toward the unexpected voice and her stomach lurched. They had brought Miss Thorndike.

And of course they would! Why hadn't she thought of that? When she'd asked Del and Hari to meet her at the Egyptian Consulate she'd pictured just the three of them. But now—

"I already signed the registry for us so we shall proceed to the gallery to begin our tour. I had no idea you would be joining us, Miss Charkova." The aging governess gave Rue a sour look. "Do try to keep up."

Miss Thorndike swept up the girls and herded them in through the door marked 'Museum Gallery'. She marched straight to the registration desk and picked up the pen. With a flourish she added a new line to the list of museum visitors, then turned to lead the way into the hall.

As they passed, Rue leaned toward the desk to get a closer

look at the registry. On the last line she clearly read two words. *Russian Chit.*

The woman knew her name but couldn't be bothered to write it. The insult was bruising. But was it a good thing her name wasn't actually there? Rue dismissed the thought before it was fully formed. Anyone with half a brain could figure out who the Russian chit was who'd accompanied the Mountmarten and Wayburton girls into the museum. When they found the jewels the culprit's name would be right there. With theirs. In indelible black ink.

Or perhaps they'd think it was one of the girls who delivered the jewels and they'd be in terrible trouble and everyone would know they had to have gotten the jewels from Rue and—

Did she dare continue with her plan?

From that moment onward, the entire tour was a blur. Their guide droned on as Miss Thorndike oo'd and ah'd over the information he imparted. Del and Hari kept up a whispered conversation with Rue, sharing every bit of gossip they'd heard in the days since they'd last been together. All she could do was nod and try to smile.

After surviving a cup of thick black Egyptian coffee in the tea room, all four women visited the washroom, and there Rue saw her chance. While the other three perfumed themselves, and tipped the attendant, Rue slipped her packet behind a stack of pristine white hand towels. It was a rash move, and her heart hammered as she thought of the many ways she was making it all too easy for them to discover who had left the jewels.

It was a terribly risky thing to do, but as she reached to snatch the packet back, her hands faltered. She couldn't bring herself to touch the things again.

She backed away from the shelf. Could she really leave them here? Did she dare?

As her mind churned with worry, Rue allowed herself to be ushered out of the consulate and back onto the avenue. She saw the worry in her friends' eyes. They were concerned by what they were seeing. She knew she appeared fearful, agitated. With immense effort, she settled herself.

"Write us from the train, dear Rue! We can't wait to hear all about your trip home!"

"Don't leave until you hear from me," Del whispered.

That loosened a tear, and Rue felt it roll down her cheek. Sweet, innocent Hari thought Rue was just another bride sailing off to marry her prince. Only Del knew the truth. Only Del could understand her desperation, could see her immense sadness at leaving her true love behind. Only Del could guess at the pain she carried in her heart.

The best she could hope for now was to be half a continent away by the time anyone found the packet of jewels.

"I suppose we must see you home, then."

While Rue stood by drowning in her sadness, Miss Thorndike began piling the girls into the Wayburton carriage. She would whisk them away, back to their world of dancing lessons and musicales and dashing young men in evening dress. It was cruel. Too cruel. So cruel that a heart might not survive it.

Rue turned to hide her tears and was stopped by a hand on her shoulder.

"Into the carriage with you now. Don't keep us waiting."

Miss Thorndike stood by, evidently expecting to escort her back to Halvord House and clearly not pleased about doing so. And while being with her friends had been immeasurably comforting, the thought of parting all over again was just too much.

"No, I...my mama iss just across street. I join her."

Miss Thorndike looked across the avenue, and seeing an assortment of shops must have decided it was safe to leave Rue to her mother's devices.

"Well then, mind the street."

Rue nodded, caught in a maelstrom of emotion over seeing her dear new friends for the last time. She had to get away before she completely shamed herself with a spate of hysterics right here on the street. But Miss Thorndike turned back toward her with a startled exclamation.

"I nearly forgot. Here's your packet. You left it in the washroom. You really should be more careful, you know."

~~~

It was like some kind of curse, finding the packet of jewels in her hands yet again. The feel of it burned through her kid gloves as if taunting her. It would not have surprised Rue at all if the blasted thing had burst into flame.

"Why you not leave me alone!"

She turned away from the street, fearful someone would see this madwoman shrieking at a brown paper package. Blinded by her confusion as to what to do next, she stumbled. Rue looked up from the packet to see what was in her way and found her path was blocked by a pile of brick and stone rubble. Two shovels lay nearby, and a bit further on several stonemasons worked on the construction of a small fountain.

Rue gasped. It seemed providential, as if the gods had seen

her plight and prepared the very hiding place she desperately sought. The pile of rubble lay just inches from her feet, with a large area scooped away, creating a natural cave-like hole in the pile. In an instant she knew it was meant for her.

But the hole was large, and it would take a lot of scooping for her to adequately cover the package of jewels. After a moment's hesitation, Rue slipped off her red shawl and dropped it into the hole, half-filling it up. Then came the package. The sight of her red shawl there in the dirt tore at her heart. But she was leaving Ned behind, and now the shawl would be left behind, as well. With the toe of her half-boot she flipped the shawl's edges over the package, and with several more kicks she dislodged enough rocks to cover the shawl and adequately fill the hole.

As she worked, she kept watch over her shoulder. The pile was on the far side of the fountain from the workmen, and they had not seen her. No foot traffic had passed close by. No heads had swiveled to see what the crazy woman was doing kicking at a mound of dirt.

She'd managed to rid herself of the jewels once and for all. In broad daylight. In the middle of London. And nobody had seemed to care a whit.

For the first time in long minutes Rue drew a breath.

She walked several paces down the avenue and hailed a cab.

"Halvord House," she told the driver, as if she were a normal customer on a normal day.

At least it was done now. Rue could only be grateful for that. But she knew without a doubt that the jewels weren't the only thing she'd buried today. She'd buried her innocence, her pride, her integrity. Her precious red shawl. It couldn't have hurt worse if she'd buried her own wretched heart.

And perhaps she had.

CHAPTER EIGHTEEN

WHAT A FOOL SHE WAS!

What an idiot to have just dropped the jewels and kicked some rocks over them and called it done. What had she been thinking? And to leave her red shawl? Bozhe moy! The register read 'Russian chit', and everyone in Mayfair had seen the Russian chit trotting about in broad daylight wearing the garish thing. Half of Society would recognize immediately that it was the very girl who'd floated about on the arm of the Duke of Wellbury. And they'd waste no time at all sharing that revelation with the other half of the ton.

And what about Del? And Hari? And Miss Thorndike? Especially Miss Thorndike. They'd witnessed her carrying a packet. If it got into the newspaper that the brown paper packet of jewels had been found wrapped in a red shawl, her friends would have no choice but to suspect her.

With her stomach tied in knots, Rue sought a powder to relieve her headache. Her mother was pouting again and Rue couldn't even muster the energy to be kind to her. Del's note that arrived that afternoon had taken care of that. Her words had sent Rue plummeting even deeper into the miserable doldrums of despair.

Ned was back in London. Early. And had been here for four whole days already. He'd made several evening appearances, but not once had he approached Del or her mother. According to Del, she had tried to waylay the duke at some affair, but he had rebuffed her.

Rue's heart sank at the thought of it. Ned knew Del was her dearest friend. If he had any desire to know where Rue was or how she might be faring, he would ask Del. She'd be the first person he would think of.

But he'd rebuffed Del, and in doing so, he'd rebuffed Rue. Indeed, it felt more like a rebuke. And it stung like nothing she'd ever experienced.

Rue sagged into a chair by the window which offered little to lift her mood. The drizzle had turned to rain, effectively sealing in the gagging smell of the tannery. Rue held a perfumed handkerchief to her nose, but it helped little.

Four days ago she'd thought there was still hope. But knowing that all the while Ned had been happily resuming his former life—and evidently doing so without a care for her—Rue was beginning to revise her thinking.

Hope was for silly children who couldn't read the facts. And the facts told her that holding out any hope of seeing Ned again was sheer folly. Her father would be proud of her for separating emotion from fact and examining the evidence in the cold light of day.

Two months in London had opened her heart to one of the greatest joys she'd known in her young life. And just as quickly it had shown her its greatest sorrow. She needed to be done with this place. She needed to redefine her world. But in a way of her own choosing.

Rue picked up the timetable that showed the Channel crossing schedule. Her mother had circled a date one week from today. It was too long to wait. She needed to leave this unhappy place before it completely destroyed her.

"Take this to change ticket, *mamochka.*"

Katerina looked at the timetable her daughter held and grew immediately angry. "*Nyet!* I will not stay longer." She knelt beside Rue's chair. "Rusilla, my precious one, how many times do I say I'm sorry? You must forgive me. And you must forget him. Do not punish me more!"

Rue sighed.

"Take this to change ticket, *mamochka.* We leave tomorrow."

~~~

Ned paid the porter who delivered the last of his cargo from the ship. He'd brought gifts for his family—tooled leather, jewelry, and several bolts of Egypt's fine cotton. It should have helped him shake off the mood that still enveloped him. But it didn't. Four days back in London and his thoughts were as turbulent as they had been when he left. *Damn and blast.* He'd been so impatient to get back to London. And for what?

For certain, being part of the delegation had turned out to be an important endeavor for him. He'd held his own among the aging dignitaries, and indeed, they'd found some of his ideas interesting. Some had even drawn him into debate and eventually come around to his side—which was always the side that posed the greater benefit for England's working class.

Georgi and Sol had driven him half mad, disappearing just when they were needed and leaving him to pick up the diplomatic pieces. He knew he should be glad for his friends, and on some level he was. But the scene Georgi had created in the Wayburton foyer had turned a most precious moment with Rue dark and malevolent, and he could not truly forgive her for it.

The matching white tigers had been well-received, and the festivities more grand than he could possibly have expected. He should be feeling the puffed chest of success. Instead, over, under, around and through every minute of every day boiled the troubling memory of how he'd left things with Rue. At two weeks into his mission he'd felt awash with shame and sent her several letters, apologizing for his horrid treatment of her and expressing his hope that they could meet as soon as he returned.

He'd desperately needed to speak to her, to see her face, watch her reaction to his words. Soften them with a caress here and there. And if she would let him, with a kiss.

But that was impossible now.

She hadn't even read them.

Because she was already gone.

A breeze ruffled the papers that cluttered his desk and he reached to capture them. His hand fell upon the note from Lady Wayburton. He'd found it among the stack of correspondence awaiting his return. On first reading he had felt hurt. Now her note just made him angry. The woman had certainly taken no pains to soften the blow.

> *Your Grace,*
> *You will, of course, already know of Miss Charkova's*
> *return to Russia. I can only say that had I known*

*her to be capable of such chicanery I should never
have kept her and her mother beneath my roof. It is
so sad when one attempts an act of kindness and is
rewarded with wickedness. I simply wish to assure
you that Wayburton and I in no way hold you re-
sponsible for the acts of a wayward foreigner.*

Faithfully yours,
Lady Rosella Wayburton

Ned crushed the note. How dare she speak so cruelly and
with such certainty? How could she know any better than anyone else if Rue was guilty? He had read his sweetheart's face,
searched her eyes, and regardless of his subsequent actions, he
now believed her.

Each time he recalled that awful night in Wayburton House
he cringed. He could still see her face as clearly as if she stood
before him. She'd been truly and honestly shocked by Georgi's
accusation. How could he not have seen it? She had no more
stolen those jewels than he had. He knew that now.

He'd known it for days. In fact, his urgent need to see her had
affected him so strongly that he'd booked an early return and
shortened his trip home by more than four days. The rest of his
group could dilly-dally with the Pasha, but he had a message to
convey—and not one that could be conveyed with mere written words. This message needed to be imparted in a far more
intimate fashion.

And then yesterday the newspapers had been full of the
discovery. Somehow the jewels had turned up in front of the
Egyptian Consulate, uncovered by laborers constructing a new
fountain. Ned hardly cared how they'd ended up there. He was

simply grateful the whole episode was at last resolved.

A recurring urge to defend Rue and restore her to the place she deserved in London Society made Ned suddenly restless. He rose from his chair and left the house. If he could have a hand in proving her innocence, he would. And he knew where he would start.

"Chesterfield Gardens," he called to his driver.

The newspaper had been very clear about where the discovery of the jewels had been made. Ned wanted to see the place firsthand.

Twenty minutes later he reached the construction site, which was not as large as he'd expected. But the small fountain tucked into an alcove formed by the building's ornate façade showed promise. It was nicely situated to form a quiet respite in the midst of busy London.

From the street, two laborers could be seen working on the fountain, clearly administering finishing touches. Ned alighted from the carriage and hailed the two men.

"I wonder if I might ask you a question," he began, "if it's not too much trouble."

One of the men stepped forward, removing his cap and wiping his brow with his sleeve. "How can I help, gov?"

"Were you here when they found the jewels?"

The man smiled. "Were I here? I were the one what found 'em." He turned to point to the area they had just cleared. "Right there, they were. Under two stone o' rubble."

Ned nodded and walked closer. "In a box, were they?"

"Naw." The fellow shook his head and smiled.

"A container with any markings on it?"

Ned had hoped he might discover a clue that would cement

in his mind what kind of person might have helped themselves to the jewels neither he nor Sol had been able to locate.

"Naw, nothin' like that. They was just wrapped up in brown paper. Oh, and that old thing."

The man pointed to an opening beneath the building's steps where a small child played. She sat on the ground, trotting a small wooden horse about on her blanket. Ned stepped out of the sun and into the shade, bent on getting a better look at the blanket.

As he drew closer and leaned forward a bit, he saw that he'd been wrong. Terribly wrong.

It wasn't a blanket at all.

It was Rue's red gypsy shawl.

~~~

Never had anything plagued him so. Rue may have sworn it wasn't her who stole the jewels, but she sure as bloody hell was the one who returned them. There could be no denying it.

It had taken quite a bit of convincing for the little girl to accept his shiny sixpence in exchange for the shawl. But he'd persisted, and once he added a big halfpenny, she relented with a smile. Now the shawl sat on the corner of his desk, taunting him.

In frustration, Ned grabbed the thing and lobbed it across the room. He couldn't look at it without seeing its long fringe dancing about Rue as she walked.

His thoughts that had begun to settle were once again in turmoil. It *was* her. He'd set out to prove her innocence and done the exact opposite. But perhaps that's what he needed to do to get her and the bloody jewels out of his thoughts once and for all. He had work to do, and now that he knew the truth he could put the whole mess behind him.

An unfinished report lay before him on his desk, the report the Queen was waiting for. She'd wanted every detail and Ned was anxious to provide them. The devil of it was, everything he'd done in Egypt, every market he'd visited, every temple and ruin, ended up reminding him of Rue. There would always be something—a woman's cheery laughter, a pretty sari made sheer by a flickering lamp. Trying to distill the actual detail from his tainted memory was like separating cream from milk. Some bit of it always stuck where it didn't belong.

The hall clock chimed the hour, reminding Ned he was due at the Albion to see Georgi and Sol off to America. He braced himself for a long afternoon. The couple was so in love they would scarcely notice anyone else in the room, and it was hard to see them so happy when he had lost all hope of ever finding happiness again.

~~~

"Buck up, old man. You'll get through this."

Solomon Rockefeller clapped Ned on the shoulder and sighed. "You're taking it too hard, my friend. Go easy on yourself. Go to Russia. Find the girl. Live your life."

After a celebratory meal at the Albion, Sol and Ned shared a glass of cognac and a cigar while they waited for Georgi to change into her traveling clothes.

"But it was her red shawl, Sol. It had to be her who put the jewels in that pile of rock."

"Maybe." Sol puffed once on his cigar. "Maybe not. It might have been a look-alike."

"Oh come now."

"No, seriously. We don't know if she had the shawl during that timeframe or not, now do we?"

"Well..."

"So, anyone in the Wayburton household might have taken it."

"Well, that is just a hair-brained fancy."

"I mean it, Ned. Let's say Devan Maclyn took the stones that night. A servant from his household bribes a servant from the Wayburton house to get the shawl, bury the jewels, make it look like Rue did it."

"That sounds like something out of a penny dreadful. Besides, Maclyn would never do that."

"What? Bribe a household servant?"

"No. Give up the jewels."

Ned took a long draw on his cigar.

"Only a guilty person returns something like that. Anonymously. For no reward."

"Or an innocent person who is protecting a guilty person."

Ned thought about that.

"Hm."

"See what I'm saying?"

"Hm. Maybe."

"I'm saying—"

"I know very well what you're saying. You're supposing that Katerina Charkova is the one who took the gems from *Rosehaven*, and when Rue discovered it, she returned them so no one is the wiser."

"Good show, Your Grace. An innocent person protecting the guilty one."

"Mm-hm."

Sol leaned forward. "But gems notwithstanding, there's a bigger problem here."

Ned laid his cigar aside. "What's that?"

"You're in love with her."

Ned couldn't even react. It was one thing to recognize the thing growing in your own heart, but it was entirely another for it to be so strong that another person could see it as well.

Ned reached for his pocket watch to stall. He had no answer for Sol. But he had one for himself.

The bloody American was bloody right.

CHAPTER NINETEEN

IT WAS TORTURE FOLLOWING HER MOTHER across the pier, but with each step Rue forced herself to accept this new path. Exile was her self-imposed sentence.

"Wait here, my daughter. I will arrange for our luggage."

Katerina began to move toward the Purser's Office and then turned to crush her daughter in an unexpected hug. "Oh my *dragotsennyy*, my precious one. We are free! No more bitter tongues and jealous granddaughters. We go home to our new life!" She drew back with a tsk. "Though how we will manage without the dowry jewels I don't—"

"*Mamochka!*"

Rue silenced her mother with a glare that took no effort at all to summon.

Her mother's excessively dramatic words touched a nerve, however. Did her mother feel no guilt? No shame? Had she already forgotten that it was her action that had robbed Rue of her dream? Rue might have stayed until Ned returned from Egypt, might have found a way to regain his trust. But now her dream seemed like a cruel hoax. Ned's silence spoke louder than any whispered hope could possibly overcome. He had cut her from his life. Anything she said now would fall upon deaf ears.

But worse, she would always bear her own guilt. Thanks to her mother's thoughtless act.

Just steps away a newsboy barked the morning headline. "Mysterious Stones of Saqqarah Recovered! Read all about it!"

Rue cringed. Were those wretched stones going to follow her forever?

She dropped a coin into the newsboy's palm and took a paper. The headline screamed to her as loudly as the boy had. But it was the bold subheading that told her what she wanted to know.

Laborers find missing jewels at fountain construction site.

The story occupied three ample columns outlining the history of the stones. It spoke sketchily of Lord Rathmore's good intentions with his ill-fated expedition. And the article's closing words cast subtle shadows of suspicion over a foreign mother and daughter who could not be located for comment.

With great effort, Rue managed to quell the shaking of her hands long enough to read the rest.

> *Early yesterday, laborers preparing the base for the new fountain at Chesterfield Gardens discovered a treasure that has been missing for over three hundred years. Two large emeralds and a cache of major diamonds taken three centuries ago from an Egyptian tomb were found hidden within a pile of rocks intended to line the fountain's foundation. The gemstones, currently being authenticated, are thought to be worth more than £145,000. They*

*are being safeguarded by the Ministry of Culture
at the Egyptian Consulate which occupies the
grounds. How the gems came to be placed there is
not yet known.*

Rue let out a shuddering breath. There was no mention of
the red shawl in which the gems had been wrapped.

Rue tossed away the newspaper, unable to dispel the thought
that she had tossed away with it the best part of her life. Ned
would know what she'd done. Others wouldn't guess, but he
would. She reached into her reticule for a handkerchief and felt
the envelope that she had not yet posted.

In the sleepless hours of her last night in London, Rue had
paced their wretched little room, searching for words to explain her actions. She'd delayed her mother as long as possible,
waiting for Ned to return from Egypt. But when he returned
and made no attempt to contact her, she had known his heart
was permanently closed to her. She'd made it so easy for him
to find her, too. All he had to do was tell Del Wayburton he
wished to see Rue and she would get them together.

Each hour had been agony as Rue had waited on tenterhooks
for a note from Del telling her where Ned wanted to meet.
Praying that he would, and fearing that he wouldn't. She began
to despair, hoping she was wrong. But as Del began to report
his presence at various social events, the wrenching truth hit
home. He was cutting her from his life. And she must accept it.

By that time she had used up most of the stationery Del had
provided for her in the small brown bundle. But there was one
sheet left, and she had easily known to whom this last letter
must go.

Sitting with pen poised above paper at the table in Halvord House she had at last begun to write. It was a garbled mess of confession and regret, but it was the truth. At the very least it was what she owed her Neddie. The truth.

Now that letter lay tucked into her reticule, waiting for her to summon the courage to post it. She could do that now, or when they reached Odessa. Or perhaps St. Petersburg. Or perhaps never.

~~~

This feeling of disquiet was new to Ned. His life had been so ordered, so understood, that he never truly had moments of confusion over the course he would take. Never.

Until he met Rusilla Ivanovna Charkova.

His steps carried him through a flock of seabirds as he returned to his carriage after seeing Georgi and Sol off. But he scarcely noticed their squawking and flapping.

There had to be something significant about that—about the fact that one slip of a girl could so thoroughly disrupt his life. Ned's step slowed as the thought took root in his troubled brain. It was she who had pulled him off course. She who had blossomed within the space he'd thought for so long he'd been reserving for Georgi.

Bloody hell.

She hadn't just blossomed within it. She'd burst the edges of it, overflowed the boundaries of it, until the essence of Rusilla filled every bit of bone and marrow within him. The thought of carrying that essence with him for the rest of his life without having her there in the flesh beside him struck a pain in Ned's heart that stunned him.

He stopped and turned his face toward the water, welcoming the buffeting breeze that cooled his brow. Ned removed his hat and ran a hand through his hair, and as he did, the very thing that troubled him seemed to fly away with the wind.

Whatever part Rue played in the finding and losing of the *Stones of Saqqarah*, he could forgive.

As soon as the thought formed, he shook it off. He needn't forgive it. Forgiving meant she bore some guilt, and he would not believe her guilty unless she told him herself that she had taken the blasted things.

Sol was right. Ned was in love with the girl. More in love than he would have thought possible. But even more, he was in need of her. In want of her.

It was powerful. Overwhelming. And consuming.

Ned was overtaken with a knowledge that there was one thing he must do. He turned and strode toward his carriage, the plan tumbling out as he walked. He would get back to Wellbury Place, put his business in order, pack a bag, and leave. Whatever it took, he would find her.

And he would never return to London without Rusilla Ivanovna Charkova at his side.

~~~

Rue felt the weight of loss settle painfully upon her. It crept downward, pressing brutally on her chest and dragging her shoulders down until she felt her whole body being drawn toward the earth. What kind of life lay ahead for her without her Neddie? Was she destined to hobble through her days like some forlorn widow? Avoiding gatherings because laughter reminded her of Ned? Avoiding music because the melody might sing of her loss?

And how could she leave London? Leave Ned? Knowing they all suspected her of a crime in which she'd taken no part except to resolve it? How could she leave Ned without one last explanation? Did she dare find him and beg him to listen? Perhaps if she did, once she laid her soul bare she might be able to read in his face if love still lived there.

Rue turned to her mother who was chattering on about some inane plan of hers.

"*Mamochka.*"

Her mother just nattered on.

"*Mamochka*, listen to this daughter."

At last her mother turned to listen.

"What is it, my *dragotsennyy?*"

"I will not go with you."

"What? This iss not possible. I cannot leave you in this wicked place." Her mother turned away. "Come. Get yourself together. It is time to go now."

As if that's all it would take to get her silly daughter in line, Katerina began to move toward the boarding area.

But Rue would not move. "I not go with you, *mamochka*. I must to fix this thing."

Her mother lapsed into Russian, issuing a spate of orders and pleas. But Rue merely turned away to face the water. The breeze that ruffled her bonnet seemed to quiet her thoughts and muffle her mother's voice.

In the distance, a flock of seabirds suddenly lifted off the pier and took flight out over the water. Their graceful wings seemed to soothe her agitation.

As she watched, a movement at the edge of the pier drew her eye. People passed back and forth before her, walking with a purpose toward carriages and gangplanks. But in the distance, a man separated himself from the crowd and followed the birds. He stopped at the edge of the pier and watched.

The line of his shoulders seemed somehow familiar. And when he took off his hat and drew a hand threw his hair, Rue gasped. It was a move she'd seen a thousand times.

Could it be?

Rue stepped off the boardwalk and into the crowd, determined to get a closer look. She was being silly, of course. What reason would Ned have to be here? Today? But she needed to know.

As the crowd became thicker, she became more bold and quickened her pace. Nearer and nearer she came, until at last she broke through, knowing she would be mere steps from where the man stood.

But he was gone.

Rue whirled about, peering in every direction, hoping to see where the man had gone.

But it was no use. There was no sign of the man. No sign of Ned. Just a few birds circling back to land on the jetty. And people behind her still moving with a purpose. Sharing happy reunions and joyful farewells.

Her heart sank.

As ridiculous as it seemed, she felt his presence. Knew he had been here. Her Neddie. Her love.

"Rue?"

She could even hear his voice.

"Rue? Is it you?"

She knew the voice was only in her head but turned toward it anyway.

And there he was.

Her Ned.

Just steps away.

Standing there with an incredulous look on his face.

"They said you were already gone."

Rue swallowed her tears.

"I wait for you, my Neddie. But…"

Ned took four quick steps and grasped her arms. "Sh. Don't speak. Just…"

"My Neddie, I…"

"Shh!" He placed a finger against her lips, and then his thumb traced them, as if his hand might confirm what his eyes were seeing.

He only spoke two words before his lips found hers.

"My love."

They echoed in her head, swirling about and banishing any fears that remained.

My love.

He clutched her fiercely as she wrapped her arms around his neck. They turned and kissed, kissed and turned, unable to stop.

"I could not leave, my Neddie," she whispered at last. "I could not leave you."

"I was coming to find you, my love," he whispered back.

His words revealed their common purpose, but it was his hands, his eyes, the way they drank her in that revealed what she needed to see. Needed to feel.

He loved her with his whole heart. And she loved him.

It was truly all that mattered.

And all that she would ever need to know.

Chapter Twenty

"My Neddie, what means this word bliss?"

Rue pulled the red shawl about her. It was always nearby here in their bedroom, but since their wedding night it had never again been seen in public.

"Hmm. Bliss? That's an easy one," he murmured.

With one finger he gently tugged the shawl away and kissed the cool flesh he'd laid bare.

"This," he growled, "is bliss."

"Oh!" Rue gasped. "Then remind this wife never use this word!"

Now Ned laughed.

"No, dearest. Bliss is the feeling that something is perfect. Something makes you perfectly happy. Something makes you supremely content. Something is—"

Rue stopped him.

"Ah. Yes. I understand now. Like chocolate."

"Mm. Yes."

"Or bliss like naked feet in grass on sunny day."

"Mm. Definitely yes."

"Or bliss like wearing new gown this afternoon."

"Well, that might be taking it a bit far. Besides, I thought we might just stay home and—"

"What?!" Rue tugged the shawl back into place. "But my Neddie, you promise."

Ned rolled off the bed and finished dressing.

"Maybe you should give it more time, my love. Let people forget all about things."

Rue contemplated what he said. He was almost always right, and in the few weeks they'd been married she had learned to listen carefully to his suggestions. But in some things, her own instincts rose above his advice and could not be ignored.

"Memory of *ton* iss long. Long. Very long. Like elephant. I think today iss day to begin their forgetting." She turned a rather coquettish look upon her husband as she reached to adjust his collar. "Yes?"

"Darling, I love our life, just the two of us. Why should we bother with the rest of the world when there is no need?"

Rue drew back. "No need? My Neddie, you not think right. You fine to go where you like. Rue, not so much. Iss why I want to fix. See, they know I not take jewels now. You make that happen. That iss good, no? But little twit is thing they cannot forget. I make new memory for them maybe they easier to forget old mistake. No?"

She had tried hard to keep the pout from her voice, but it was a sore issue. Living the rest of her life in seclusion, even with her precious Neddie, seemed like cowardice. And nobody could ever accuse Rusilla Ivanovna Charkova of cowardice. She'd never been afraid to face down her foes and she wouldn't start now.

She turned back to say more but stopped. Ned stood still in the center of the room with an expression she'd never seen before on his face.

"What?"

His silence made her nervous.

"What I say, my Neddie?"

Ned stepped to her and put a hand on each of her arms. "You're so right, my little Russian butter knife." He kissed her lightly. "I was not thinking right." His hands moved to cup her face. "You're the bravest woman I know, and if you are ready to face Society, then I shall be right there. At your side." He bent down to kiss her. "This afternoon."

Rue beamed. She'd known he would see her need. He always did. And today the two of them would make their debut in Society as man and wife. It scared her to death. But she was prepared to do whatever it took to make him proud.

She dared to do nothing less.

~~~

"Maybe you should reconsider, Rue. Just wait a little longer—"

Ned swept a harried hand through the pesky strands of hair that kept falling across his brow. Rue was turned so that she had her back to the Strothfield's gaming parlor, but beyond her head Ned could see the angry group of young people who were already staring daggers at her. They'd expected him to come alone.

He'd brought her to this afternoon social because she'd insisted. As duke he could command some respect for her. But if he took the lead, then nothing would be gained. Yet hanging back and watching her enter the fray alone had him second guessing their decision. Earlier he'd agreed that this was the perfect opportunity to break some of the ice that had crystallized into a wall between Rue and the *beau monde*. Between his lovely Russian belle and London's elite, the beautiful ones. The ones who with a slight raise of an eyebrow could dash a poor girl's hopes.

But now he feared for her. He knew how cutting they could be, how easily they could slice an ego in half.

"Iss time, my Neddie. For once and for all time I must do this thing. I must fix. You come with Rue now."

Before he could protest, she took his arm and drew him into the parlor. Her trembling hand told him how fearful she was, but her straight back and lifted chin spoke of her courage in facing the group who had scant weeks earlier been so cruel.

The four couples gathered around the parlor card table suddenly quieted. He could see their hesitation as to how to greet the newcomers. They saw him—a respected member of Parliament, a duke whose title was centuries old. And her—a foreigner, a pariah. An outcast.

As he and Rue drew to a stop near the table, one young earl stood and the other three gentlemen followed suit. "Your Grace," they said with a deferential nod, offering him the respect he was due. They mumbled Rue's name in greeting, though none looked her direction as they spoke. The young ladies gave their gushing greetings to Ned and didn't even pretend to greet Rue.

If he had his way, these derelict wastrels would be sent to bed with no supper. Ned ground his teeth, fearful his true thoughts might just explode from his mouth.

But it was Rue who spoke first.

"Iss room for one more little twit?"

Ned cringed as each face at the table arranged itself into a vision of hostility. On the opposite side of the table, Lady Eugenia Strothfield shot to her feet.

"How dare you come here like this!"

Rue's hand clutched Ned's arm as if she feared she might fall. "I come to give you chance to say bad thing to me, Lady Eugenia. To my face. I...I deserve such bad thing."

Now her whole body trembled, but she stood resolute. Ned placed his free right hand on top of Rue's hand that clutched feverishly at his left sleeve.

Outwardly she seemed marvelously composed, not showing a bit of her nerves to the world. Only to him.

Now she stepped away from Ned and faced Eugenia.

"You to say bad thing to me. I ready."

God forbid! She doesn't know what she's asking!

Ned was aghast that Rue would do such a thing. She'd walked right up and invited these churlish children to hurl their worst insults. And there wasn't a bloody thing he could do about it.

Eugenia stalked a bit closer. "A bad thing, eh? I should call you something like...*twit*?" She twirled a ringlet with her finger as she contemplated Rue's request. "I'm not sure there's anything worse. Oh wait! In fact there is." She took another step toward Rue. "You, Miss Charkova, are a *minging vazey whooperup!*"

All seven of her companions gasped in unison. It was so very shocking to hear such gutter language from a cultured lady.

But Rue didn't even flinch. She merely turned to Ned and raised her eyebrows in curiosity. "What means *minging*?"

Ned coughed. "It, well, it means, um—"

"It means foul. Or smelly," Eugenia interrupted archly.

Now Rue looked startled. "I smelly? Truly? I—"

"No, Rue. She's just insulting you. To make you feel bad. Like you asked." Ned stepped a bit closer to Rue, searching his mind as to what he might do to diffuse the situation. But Rue was determined to see it through.

"Ah. Yes. Insult is what I want. And, um, what *vay-zee* means?"

"Stupid." Ned said quietly.

"Ah. I admit I stupid." Rue frowned. "But this *hoodle nut*? Vat iss this?"

"*Whooperup*," half the voices at the table offered, then looked a bit sheepish.

"Yes. *Whooperup*. This means?"

Now everyone at the table was silent, until at last one bold miss spoke up. "It means second rate singer, someone who produces noise instead of music. Like a tavern singer."

Rue gasped and Ned was distraught to see shame spill across her face. How could this vindictive woman criticize the finest musical talent Ned had heard in London? It was harsh. Too harsh. Too personal. He would put a stop to this. "I say, that's quite enough—"

But Rue's pained words trampled his.

"You not like my music! I so sorry!" She threw both hands over her mouth, but not before a single tear slid down her cheek. "I so sorry!"

She turned her shoulders toward the door as if she would flee the room, but Lady Eugenia rushed forward and caught her. "I didn't mean it!" she wailed. "I love your music. Your...your voice is beautiful! And that, that thing you played, your—" She searched for a word to describe Rue's instrument.

"My balalaika?"

"Yes! Your—oh heavens, I can't even pronounce it much less play such a thing." Lady Eugenia sighed. "This has grown way out of hand, Miss Charkova. I never really minded being your little twit, but Grandmama, well, you know how she is. Please, please forgive me!" She threw her arms wide, waiting for Rue to step into her hug.

Rue hesitated. Ned feared the criticism had been too piercing, too hurtful for her to recover quickly. And then he saw mischief invade her eyes.

"My little *twit* not know to say *balalaika?*" She made a dramatic sigh. "This *hooper-duck* too *vay-zee* to understand how this can be." Rue made great fun of herself, then grinned and stepped into the hug, her laugh joining Eugenia's as they shared their relief to be done with the whole debacle.

Ned watched, amazed. They'd been ready to draw daggers just moments earlier and now, with a few sincere, self-deprecating words, it was as if nothing had ever happened.

"Now," Rue said as she took Lady Eugenia by the hand. "I teach you old Russian card game. Iss called *Durak*."

Ned drew back a chair for Rue who had already swept up a loose deck of cards and was masterfully shuffling it into place. As he found his own seat across from her, Rue was already calling out the rules of the game, including a modern innovation which had partners switching chairs each time their hand came up empty. They had to rush around the table and be seated before the next card was laid. The one who didn't quite make became, for the next play or two, the *durak*.

Just as the table was set to play, a young dandy spoke up. "You must tell us, Miss Charkova. What does *durak* mean?"

Rue sat back in her chair. "You not need to know this, my friends. Ready?"

"No, really," the young man persisted. "We want to know."

The entire table chimed in, begging for an answer.

"Well," she said as she swept her eyes around the table. "Iss mean *fool*."

The laughter died as quickly as smiles faded. Ned held his breath as he watched the small group realize they'd just been drawn into a game of Fool. And then the most remarkable thing happened. Lady Eugenia gasped, laughed prettily, and began to applaud. "I simply love it! Let's begin!"

It was more than a marvel to Ned, how easily the table joined in the bungling hilarity once the tension was well and surely banished. They laughed, they crowed, they screamed with delight when one of them ended up the "fool".

Without a doubt it was Rue who presided over the table. Rue who steered the game so that wonder of wonders, each of the young people had their turn at playing the fool. Even Ned.

But it wasn't until late into the afternoon that he realized the only person who had not yet fallen to the fool's gambit was Rue.

~~~

The next morning Ned begged for some time in his office. Papers were piling up and much research had to be done if he didn't intend to become the laughing stock of Parliament.

"Really, darling. An hour is all I ask. Then we shall take the carriage and promenade. Just an hour. Promise." He sealed his promise with a kiss.

"One hour, my Neddie. Iss all I can stand, this wife thinks."

She danced away and left him at his study door. He would make it one hour on the dot, knowing he could barely last that long away from her either.

But an hour later he wasn't quite finished with his work. Still, he'd promised her, so he left his desk to beg just thirty more minutes. After a brief search he found her in the solarium.

"Oh! My Neddie! Iss hour already?"

Rue jumped up from the table where she was working and gave him the kiss he was waiting for.

"What is all this?" he asked as he gestured to the pile of notes she'd been concentrating on.

"This?"

Rue gave a wide sweep of her arm to indicate the table, then swept up a few of the notes and struck a most coquettish pose.

"These, my darling Neddie, are invitations. Tea parties, lawn parties, and four dinner engagements. And that iss just some. Iss wonderful!"

Ned stepped closer and saw that it was true. Half the *ton* seemed bent upon entertaining the Duke and Duchess of Wellbury. It seemed that once Lady Eugenia reconciled with Rue, the rest of her friends fell all over themselves to include Rue.

"Am I to believe we are to attend these? All of these?" Ned could see his future being swept completely out of his hands.

"Yes, my Neddie, all of them!"

He couldn't help but grin, seeing her face lit so beautifully by that joyous smile.

"Really, darling, can't you refuse even a few of them?"

A shocked expression played across her face as she slowly shook her head.

"Oh no, my Neddie. I could not dare to do that."

"Well, then, I suppose we shall have to accept them all. But you must make me a promise."

"Anything, my Neddie."

"You must promise not to come home too exhausted for—"

"Oh my Neddie. What means this word?"

"Exhausted? Well, tired. Weary. Ready to fall asleep."

A curious smile spread her lips wide.

"Then I ask, my Neddie, too tired for what?"

She stepped to him and let her fingers play with his waistcoat.

"Too tired for...me," Ned growled as he pulled her into his arms.

"Too tired for you?"

Rue slipped a hand behind his neck and drew him down to her for a kiss.

"Oh no, my husband. I will never be too tired for you."

She kissed him in a wanton way that had his heart pounding and his head spinning.

And when at last she had well and truly sealed her promise, she drew back and winked.

"This wife would not dare."

TRANSLATIONS:

Bozhe moy!	My God!
dragotsennyy	precious
mamochka	mama, mommy
durak	fool
Podozhdite minutku!	Wait a minute!
zaychik	little bunny
nyet	no
da	yes
Pomni svoye obeshchaniye	Remember your promise

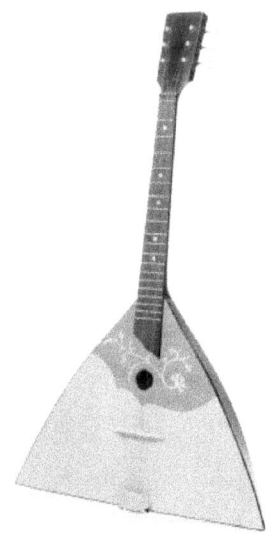

balalaika: Russian guitar

About Bailey Bristol

Bailey Bristol, author of historical romantic suspense, lives in the American Midwest. An accomplished director of opera and music theatre, retired IT geek, and devoted grandmother, Bailey promises mesmerizing characters caught up in precarious plots.

And of course, always a happy-ever-after.

MORE FROM BAILEY BRISTOL
The Samaritan Files
Love Will Follow

WRITING AS MARY SCHWANER
Courage in a White Coat

The Samaritan Files

1895
TURN-OF-THE-CENTURY
NEW YORK CITY

Bailey Bristol

LOVE
will follow

An American tale of love and grit by
Bailey Bristol

A true wartime
drama based on
the experience of
Dr. Dorothy Joy
Kinney Chambers
and her family

COURAGE
in a white coat

An American woman lives her dream...
a ten-year medical mission in India,
a fairytale marriage, and two years in the
Philippine Islands. But having survived three
years in a Japanese POW camp, she discovers
her little family could be just 24 hours from

MARY SCHWANER
with BOBBI CHAMBERS HAWK M.D.